Southern Girl

Daisy Dukes and Cowboy Boots

Eddie King

First published in Great Britain in 2015
Paperback edition published in 2015
Available as an eBook from December 2015
Parakeet Publishing, London
Printed and distributed by Ingram Spark via Lightning
Source

A CIP catalogue record for this book is available from
the British Library.

ISBN: 978-0-9935032-0-7

Dedicated to Her.

1

"Belle Meade on ice," I call out to the cute bartender as I wiggle and shake to get comfortable on the tall stool slightly left of the centre of the long brass bar. I used to be a Jack Daniel's man until I learned of the original Tennessee whiskey. The chair is at that weird height where my feet don't fully reach the ground, and if I try and rest them on the slippery footrest my knees press up against the front board. I have to look after these new knees I've got. The replacement surgery was so agonising; I never want to go through that again. Well, the actual replacement wasn't painful because I was under, but the months after were hell. You'd think that by 2059 they would have better painkillers. Problem is, if I move back, I'm too far from the bar, which is even more painful. Tall people problems, I suppose. I feel like I'm in church; I don't know whether to stand, sit, or kneel. At least this seat has a back to it though. Not all of them do. Why do they even make seats without a back? I would probably be more comfortable in one of the leather-cushioned booths, but this is the seat. It has to be this one. It always is. It always has been. Plus, if you're a lonely punter like me, even at a restaurant, it is etiquette to sit at the bar. It almost makes it acceptable to be there without any company.

The barmaid bounces over, introduces herself, Ashley, and slams my drink down in front of me. She looks like every other girl that has ever worked at this bar and is sticking to the strict uniform policy. Short shorts, comfortable shoes, and a top that would get you a tip. Man, if I was fifty-years younger. It was a smart business decision. I'm sure most of the guys come here to ogle at the barmaids in their Daisy Dukes, which seem to get shorter and shorter every year. I don't even think they're called Dukes anymore. Now they're called cut-off jeans or something like that. Whatever they're called, they are really just glorified pockets on a belt. I may be old, but I'm not complaining. Reminds me that I'm still alive. I forget sometimes. Back home, and I use that term very loosely now, the bartender would always be an intimidating, but cheeky, bald East End gangster. I prefer the bopper. I straighten up the napkin she carelessly plopped my drink on and turn the glass so that the Greenbrier logo faces away from me. I know what I'm drinking because I'm the one who ordered it, but it's important for everyone else to know. That's why they printed it on the glass, right? I'll support their promotional ploy.

Now that I am comfortable and the glass is facing the correct way, I can reach into my bag, yep, when you're my age you always carry a bag around, and pull out the picture of Madison. I often forget my medicines, but I never leave my house without her photo. I know she's gone, but I like to see her face every day. I take her with me everywhere. It makes me feel safe. It makes me feel like she's still here with me. The frame is chipped on three of the four corners, but you can't really tell unless you look closely. It blends in with the design. It probably could do with a changing, but it has safely housed this gorgeous photo ever since it was taken. A time when photos resided in frames rather than screens. It would feel wrong to change it now. When did I become so sentimental?

Madison, never Maddie, she hated that, smiles and looks straight at me. The sun has blown out the top right of her head, but the flare, or glare, whichever, blends in with her golden hair. It makes me the sad kind of happy if that makes any sense. I'm sad that she's no longer here, but just seeing her face fills my heart with endless joy.

It is expectedly quiet in the bar. It's not even noon yet and they did just open. I know it's early, but I'm only here a few times a year and it is vital I get this seat. The usual losers stroll in every ten minutes or so and gather at the end of the bar. I only label them that because it's the name of the bar. Losers. What a fantastic name for a bar. I'm surprised the Americans share that gem of humour. They have a sister bar called Winners, but that's not as funny. My main issue with that is why they call it a sister bar. Why not a brother bar, or a sibling bar, or even a cousin bar? Do you ever sit there for hours wondering why things like that are the way they are? Just me? Maybe it's because I have all this time. Nothing but time. I spend most of my days sitting, drinking tea on the porch, so I have plenty of time to dedicate to useless thoughts. Trust me, I am as surprised as them that I'm still here. I should have been gone a long time ago. I continue my ritual and make sure the frame is aligned correctly using the edge of the bar as a guide. I take a giant sip of the bourbon. Technically, it is bourbon, even though it doesn't come from Kentucky. Like my old friend Jack, maybe they should call themselves Tennessee whiskey.

A beam of sunlight swipes across the bar like a laser as another customer walks in. A slightly heavy-set fella, for English standards, but a common sight here. His average American attire: baseball cap, oversized t-shirt, shorts, white socks, fit in, but there is an air of wonderment about him. It's definitely his first time here. He looks around eagerly, evaluating his decision to choose this establishment. They all look the same. Wooden furniture, sports memorabilia displayed on the wall like it's worth something, and a hundred flat screen televisions carefully positioned to avoid any blind spots that all show different games of the sport that is in season. It's baseball season right now if you were wondering. It's never cricket season. They only jump between baseball, basketball, American football, and then would sometimes show normal football, what they call soccer, hockey, what I call ice hockey, and NASCAR, what everyone calls the redneck Formula 1. They are good at sport, and do it right, but that could be because the only sports they play, are sports that no one else in the world plays.

The young fella considers seating options. The whole bar is empty, but he ends up settling down uncomfortably close to me. He does have the courtesy to leave at least one stool between us, though. Like all of them, he is confidently loud. I suppose that's why you never see an American ninja. He tries to crack a joke with the bartender, but her wry smirk shows that she doesn't get it. She introduces herself to him and serves him a bottled beer. There I was thinking that Ashley shared her name with me because I was special. She swiftly returns to her station and gets back on her phone. From the corner of my eye, I can see him look over at me, itching to start a conversation. This makes me focus on my picture even harder, but that doesn't deter him in any way. It only gifts him a way in. Without any hesitation, he starts his investigation. "Hey, old timer? Who that in the photo you got there?"

A part of me wants to lie and a part of me doesn't want to say anything at all. I look up from the photo and stare straight ahead at the bar for a short few seconds before slowly swivelling just my head to analyse him. I fear that comes across too intimidating, so I coat it with the smallest of smiles. He takes another sip of his beer and turns his body to face me. "You look pretty sad there old timer." Is that an observation he is making out loud or a question? I don't think I look sad, even though I am a little. Is he feeling sorry for me? A sad old man drinking whiskey alone at a bar eleven o'clock in the morning staring at a picture. I feel sorry for myself.

He moves the stool separating us out of the way and shuffles his seat closer. Now there is no barrier of safety between us. He introduces himself, "Chris," and continues, "What's your story, old timer?" What's with the "old timer?" I let it slide the first two times, but is he really going to add it to the end of every sentence? I'm not even that much older than him. I thought I was only on the border of being an old timer to the young'uns. Apart from that, he seems like a pleasant enough chap. Friendly. He has a kind face that has smiled a thousand smiles. I notice that he is wearing a University of Alabama T-shirt. There will be no tides rolling here, thank you very much.

I can't be too picky these days. I'm running

out of people to talk to. I'm probably his good deed for the day. Again, "What's with the photo?" At least he didn't say… there it is. "Old timer", he presses, waiting for a response or even a reaction.

"My wife," I proudly reply. I keep it short and sweet, hoping that would be it, but also knowing very well that it won't be.

"She left you?" he knowingly enquires. Why else would I be looking at a photo of her? He doesn't wait around for an answer, turning back to face the bar and taking another shot from his bottle. "Yep, I know all about that. I was going out with my girl for two years, we were even living together. All of a sudden last week she packs up and leaves for Nashville", he pours in a more sombre tone. I process it, and then pivot to face him. I can sense a pain in his voice. He's not going to start crying, but I know he's hurt. I know that hurt. Once your heart has suffered, you not just empathise, but you want to lend an ear and share. "That's why I drove down here from Kentucky. We didn't even fight or nothing.

I just need to find her and see her, you know?" I find myself nodding like one of those bobble-head dolls. Boy, do I know. Ignoring his poor grammar, I signal Ashley to get him another beer and to top me up. I take a big sip while she fetches his bottle and tell her to top me up again. I adjust the frame and begin to tell him the story I play in my head every single day.

2

It was many years ago now. I was in London, crabbing along. That's a term I coined. Good, isn't it? You know, because crabs don't move forwards, or backwards, they kind of just shuffle sideways. So, if one is crabbing along, it means that nothing spectacular is happening in his or her life. You're at a point where you feel like you're not progressing in any part of your life. You're just crabbing along. It will catch on. Okay, so, I didn't really have anything going on. Nothing and no one excited me. I was bored. Samuel Johnson once said, "When a man is tired of London, he is tired of life; for there is in London all that life can offer", but what did he know? I disagreed with that. Maybe that were true in the 1700s, but times had changed. It was too busy, too loud, too dirty, and too expensive. It was filled to the brim, and am sure still is, with miserable sardines. Think cultured New Yorkers. I was fed up and needed to get away. I must have been in my mid to late twenties. I was in need of something different. I remember I had woken up one morning and found myself in a position where I had absolutely nothing to do. Sounds nice, but it was boring. I had a dentist appointment the following week, but that was literally it. I didn't even need a haircut.

My father had left me a couple of properties when he died, which I collected rent from. That meant I didn't really have to work. I could have, but I had everything I needed, and I was never that shrewd businessman who used that base to build a property empire. I was more focussed on getting my golf handicap into single figures, or learning how to speak Chinese. Never got too far with either. It was that time of the morning when it was too late for breakfast and too early for lunch. I thought I'd kill some time, so switched on the TV. I was flicking through the channels, and for some reason had landed on *The Hanna Montana Movie*. It was before she shaved her head and went all crazy. It was that scene where Taylor Swift performs at that typical country hoedown. Believe it or not, back then she used to be country.

It was clear I needed a holiday. I was craving something different, something exciting, something inspiring. I knew I needed to get away, but I didn't want to do the same old thing. I had been to Vegas, Dubai, Paris, the South of France, Barcelona, and Ibiza dozens of times. The best way to choose was to do what they did in the movies, spin a globe or roll out a large map and fly to wherever my finger landed. The first issue with my inspired plan was that I didn't have a globe or a map. Who actually had a globe or a large map of the world lying around? Those things became extinct decades ago. So, I opened up my laptop and went online. You'd be surprised how hard it was to get the perfect map with country and city names clearly marked in a readable font. I finally found one. I closed my eyes, spun around a couple of times and moved my extended index finger toward the laptop. I searched around for a bit then opened my eyes realising I had completely missed the screen. It always went smoother in movies. I tried again, without the spinning. Luckily, I landed on the screen. I opened my eyes to see I had drowned in the Arctic Ocean. I know seventy percent of the Earth's surface is water, so it wasn't that surprising really. Third time lucky? Turkey. Nope. It would have been nice to go somewhere they spoke English. Again. China. Nope. I tried one more time, guiding my finger to the left. Ah, America. Perfect. Without lifting my finger off the screen, I looked closer to see exactly where in the United States I'd be visiting. Tennessee. Memphis to be precise. I was an Elvis fan, but I heard that Memphis was a bit ghetto, so I convinced myself that the capital city, Nashville, counted. The whole thing was rigged anyway. I was a grown man. I was allowed to make decisions for myself. I didn't have to leave everything to fate. To make it more adventurous, I zoomed in and selected a small town outside the comforts of a big city. Not too far that I would be completely stranded in case of an emergency, but not too close either. The first one that jumped out at me was a small city called Franklin. You can't get more American sounding than Franklin, Tennessee. Just then, my attention was turned back to the television when I heard Tennessee mentioned. Turns out *The Hannah Montana Movie* was set in Tennessee. I researched it to see where exactly, and parts of it were filmed in Franklin. I mean if that's not destiny, I don't know what is. It was as simple as that.

I searched high and low for the best ticket. I always wanted to be one of those people who had brand loyalty and collected air miles, but I was too cheap for that. I'd always go for the lowest fare, so I ended up with 10,000 miles with each airline. I didn't mind if I had to stop over in a random city because it meant that I could then list it on my places visited. Plus, money saved on the flight, which was less than a tenth of my holiday, could be put towards the actual holiday. The thought of waking up the next morning at 4 a.m. kind of added to the excitement. If it were a lot cheaper, I'd even consider flying out of Gatwick. Heck, I'd sit in cargo if they let me. I had splurged on first class once to Las Vegas. It was nice, it was very nice, but it was not worth anywhere near the £10,000 I paid. You'd think for that much you would have a private room with a private bathroom with a huge hot tub where bikini-clad air stewardesses would feed you grapes and fan you with giant leaves. None of that. You all get to the same place at the same time. In fact, the middle of the plane is probably the safest part. If you crashed into a mountain, the people in first and business would get crushed, and the back of the plane would probably fall off, leaving the people in the middle without a scratch. I wouldn't say I was frugal, simply wise with my money. For example, when I was in Paris, instead of staying at a Holliday Inn for the entire stay, I would slum it in a shitty motel on the day I arrived and the days it was just me, and then book a suite at The Plaza on the weekend, when I would meet people. That way, I got to experience the finer things in life, and they would feel even finer after spending a few days at the Motel la Merde.

3

Ashley, the barmaid, interrupts me and asks us if we want another round. Of course! Keep them coming, I'm just getting started. All this talk of London has tickled my taste buds for a Guinness, but I know I will be grossly disappointed if I order one. I am yet to find a proper pint of Guinness in America. I've heard that it doesn't travel well, but I don't buy that. If we can send a man to the moon, I'm sure we can figure out a way to send Guinness to America. Once we do that, then we can worry about training up the bartenders on this continent how to pour the perfect pint. It's an art. I stick to the Belle Meade and tell her to keep the bottle close. I order another beer for the young chap. He's very thankful and is now invested in my story.

4

Where was I? Oh yeah. So, I booked my flight. I was officially flying to Nashville, Tennessee, by way of Charlotte, North Carolina. The cheapest I could find was with US Airways. I hadn't heard great things, but that didn't bother me too much. They were all the same, just with different paint on the outside. People usually booked their flights months and months in advance, but anything could happen in that time. Call me impatient, but if I felt like going somewhere, I felt like going there and then. Plus, I've noticed that prices often dropped a few days before travel. What really got me were those adverts you'd see with big bold letters reading "New York from £199," but when you called them up, it'd be closer to the £800 mark. It was never the right date, or the right airport, or the right amount of passengers, or I was wearing the wrong colour shirt. Bastards! So, I booked a flight for the very next day.

The next step was to find somewhere to stay. There weren't many Hiltons in the small town, so I started searching for alternatives. Vacation rentals were all the rage. Everyone was talking about them, so I looked for an apartment I could rent. I wanted something authentic. I found a quaint little bungalow with a beautiful front garden. 1497 Mapleberry Drive. There weren't many photos, so it was a bit of a gamble, but the description said two-bedrooms, two-bathrooms, fully fitted kitchen, etc. It was more space than I needed, but it was still cheaper than a tiny hotel room. It was almost too cheap to be true. The perfect way to really feel integrated into the local community and experience what it would be like to be a local in the foreign land, I thought. I received a message from the owner of the house with directions, instructions, and suggestions. She said that she would leave the key under the front doormat. I found that very odd. It must have been an extremely safe neighbourhood. The rest of my day filled up pretty quickly. I went and got my pre-flight massage, exchanged all of my money, bought some new shoes, and most importantly, a new box of Yorkshire Tea. I had been stuck in too many places around the world without a good cuppa, so I always took my own supply wherever I went. I expected America not to be too bad, but better safe than sorry.

I had an early flight the next morning, so I stayed up and did all my packing. The plan was that I would be super tired and be able to sleep on the long flight. My system that was yet to actually work. I almost forgot, but I thought I ought to let my neighbour, Will, know that I was going away for a few days otherwise he might have gotten worried. I wouldn't say Will and I were that close, neighbours before friends, but he would pop in every other day and drink my beer. He didn't even ask anymore. He'd stroll into the kitchen, open the fridge, and help himself. I didn't mind, though. In fact, it got to a point where I started buying the brand that he liked because he drank more of it than I did. He was older than me, but for some reason I felt responsible for him. He lived alone, but his daughter would come and stay with him during school holidays. I think he went through a messy divorce up in Newcastle or somewhere near there and moved south a few years ago. It was very early, so I felt bad waking him, but I thought I should leave him a key. There were builders working in the building, so I thought I'd better tell him to keep an eye on the apartment. He didn't work, so he wasn't too upset with the early wake-up call. I stocked up on beer before I left, to make sure he would check in as usual.

I called for a cab and made sure I was at the airport a good four hours before my flight. I always gave myself more than enough time, in case of traffic or any other delay. I hated the stress of being late and rushing more than arriving at places uncomfortably early and having to wait around. There was traffic that morning, but I still arrived at the airport more than the suggested three-hours before my flight. It was time to start queuing. The airport was just one big queue with little pit stops in between. There was a queue for everything: the check-in machine, the bag drop, security, the bar, the toilet, the plane, and then you'd sit down for ten hours only for the queue to continue on the other end with passport control, customs, and taxi. It's just one long queue.

I checked in, but I knew my bag was at least three kilos heavier than my allowance. I weighed it on my bathroom scale. The lady at the bag drop counter asked me to place the bag on the scale while she ran through the most useless security questions. Yes, I did pack the bag myself. Yes, the bag had been in my possession at all times, apart from when the taxi driver took it from me to put in the boot. No, I didn't pack any explosives. She banged away on her keyboard and then dropped the bomb on me. "You're a little overweight, sir."

I grabbed my stomach, "excuse me?"

She was quick to clarify that she meant the bag was overweight, hoping she didn't offend me. I was just joking. I thought that if I was nice and friendly, she would let it slide. She didn't have much of a sense of humour and told me that I had to either take some stuff out and put it in my hand luggage or pay a fee. I explained that I didn't have any hand luggage, hoping that would work in my favour and that she would let me off, but instead, she started giving me directions to a shop in the terminal where I could buy a carry-on bag. I tried making the argument, but ended up just paying the damn fine. That whole thing is a racket. I mean, if I carried it in my hand they wouldn't have minded, but because I was checking it in they wanted to charge me? It was going on the same plane, right? If three measly kilos made such a big difference, then they would start weighing the passengers too. I can understand if someone was taking the piss with ten extra suitcases filled with concrete bricks, but they really need to ease up on an extra bag or a few extra kilos here and there. I'm sure there were some people that didn't check anything in, so why couldn't I take some of their allowance? I hate it when companies don't operate with simple logic. It was just another way for them to make more money off me. That's how they get you. Next time I'm going to get my own back by wearing everything in my closet.

I wasn't too confrontational with her, though. I still needed to be nice because I had to sweet talk her into an exit row seat, so I could have the extra legroom. I played the 'I'm super tall' card, adding a couple of inches to my actual height. Again, she hit me with another fee and again I tried to fight my case before giving in and agreeing to pay. She typed away and then informed me that there were none available. I asked if there was anything she could do. After some more obnoxiously loud tapping on her keyboard, she said that there were a lot of business class seats left, so she could offer me one of those. A huge smile was instantly wiped from my face when she said I'd "only" have to pay a £1,200 upgrade cost. That was almost double what I paid for my economy seat. I respectfully declined, but made sure she felt my annoyance.

They were willing to let me suffer in a tight seat for ten hours when there were dozens of comfortable empty seats just metres in front of me. Was that fair? Airlines really should make accommodations for tall people. I understand that larger people sometimes had to pay for two seats, but I couldn't help being tall. It was the way I was made. Don't get me wrong, I enjoyed all the benefits that came with being tall, and would never trade it in, but travelling economy can be a real pain in the knees. It's pure discrimination against tall people and airlines should be forced to upgrade passengers over 6'3½".

At that point, I was surprised she didn't try charging me for a window seat. I know the aisle would have been better for stretching my legs, but I always found it awkward when a stranger climbed over me. At least with the window I had something to lean against and could try and get some sleep. She printed me off another boarding pass and circled the boarding time.

The next obstacle was going through security. My problem wasn't with the fact that there was security, but with the cretins who slowed down the whole process. Everyone knew you weren't allowed to take liquids in, yet people still carried large bottles of water and then acted shocked when they were asked to throw it away. I did always wonder what they would say if a smart arse left the bottle of Evian in the freezer the night before and tried carrying it across as ice. Technically that's a solid, and solids are allowed. I never liked carrying anything, so for me it was pretty simple. I emptied my pockets: passport, pen, coins, wallet, Bose headphones off from around my neck, and took off my shoes. Hence, why I bought new shoes every time I flew. They told you to take off your belt, but I never did. I reassembled myself on the other side, placing everything back in the correct pocket, and entered the bright world of duty-free. No time for stopping, I already had my destination set. I walked the long way around, looking into all the shops as I passed them, but landed at the restaurant/bar/pub/kitchen in the corner. It was like a Weatherspoon's, but maybe a tad classier. Definitely a tad more expensive. It was a staple establishment in all airports. I asked for a table in the back, and without looking at the menu, ordered a sausage bap and a pint of Stella. That's right, a beer. The airport is the only place you can order a beer at 7 a.m. without being judged. Well, there was probably a little judgement, but they didn't know what time zone I was on. I wasn't the only one drinking.

My second pint down, I checked the monitor to see what gate they had assigned. Gate 33. It was always gate 33. It was never gate 1. It always had to be the furthest gate to where I was sitting. It's as if they were trying to save fuel by making people walk the first part of the journey. A thirty-minute walk as smug airport staff zoomed past on their electric buggies. Oh, how I wanted to kick them off and steal their cart. The next half an hour sitting at the gate was mostly taken up by trying to calculate how many more pints I could have fitted in.

They invited first class passengers to board, business class, gold members, and those who needed extra time to board. After all the important people had comfortably boarded, they started boarding the common folk. "Zone 1." I looked at my boarding card, of course, I was zone 3. The lady on the speaker repeated, "Zone 1 only at this time please," which must have come out as, "Everyone in the vicinity, please stand up and gather around the desk in all directions." It was always a mess. Like it was the last helicopter out of Vietnam. I stayed seated, knowing better. The plane wasn't going to leave without me. Then again, if everyone thought like that, the plane would never leave. There would just be a bunch of people sitting down saying the plane is not going to leave without me. My section was the last to be called.

I was greeted at the door of the plane with the fakest of smiles. The stewardess looked at my pass, pointed to the right and directed me straight down the aisle. Where else could I have gone? It was hard to get lost in a straight line. The business class passengers were already working away on their laptops, looking up at the less fortunate as we paraded to the back of the plane. Taunting us, showing us that they were busy making money while we tried to squeeze two people into one seat. I located my seat and thanked the Good Lord that nobody was sitting next to me. I unfolded the blanket, put my seatbelt on the outside of it, discarded the eye mask, and stared at the people still finding their seat to see which one of the strangers I would have to be uncomfortably close to for the next ten hours. They all either sat down in front or walked on by. Was it possible that for the first time in my life, I wouldn't have anyone sitting next to me? No. Just as that thought entered my mind, an older lady made eye contact. She double checked her boarding pass, and then struggled to put her suitcase in the overhead bin. I would have helped, but I was strapped in. I could tell she was definitely English from the cross look that lived on her face. She reached into her Mary Poppins handbag and pulled out a book, a magazine, a newspaper, a crossword puzzle book, her glasses, ear plugs, her neck pillow, her own eye mask, a bottle of water, an apple, and a bag of snacks. I thought I was prepared with a pen for the customs card, but she was set for a two-week voyage. I thought about making a witty comment, but obviously I stayed silent. Her being English meant she didn't say a word either. I always waited too long to start a conversation and then it would be too late. You can't sit next to someone for an hour without saying a single word and then all of a sudden start chatting away. There is a very small window of opportunity, which I always seemed to miss. I was just about to say something, but the cabin crew started their announcements. Great British problems.

We were reminded that we weren't allowed to use the toilets reserved for the upper class, and then the curtain was pulled forward so that they didn't even have to look at us. I don't blame them. We were quite the unsightly bunch. The flight was long, boring, and cold... and we had only been in the air for about thirty minutes. The next thirty minutes were spent contemplating how I would go about reclining my seat. It was easy if the person sitting behind you got up to go to the toilet because then you could do it without them noticing, but the lady behind me wasn't moving. She even declined the free water they brought around. I looked straight ahead, didn't make any eye contact, and made the bold move to push the little button on my armrest and lean back. I felt guilty, but the person in front of me had done it, so I had no choice. Things like that always stressed me out. The next issue was my shoes. I had taken them off and placed them under the seat in front of me. There was that constant worry that they would slide around during the flight, or that I would accidentally kick them too far forward and not be able to find them at the end.

I spied the lunch cart making its way down the aisle. I took off my headphones so I could listen out for the options being offered. One was always chicken, and then there was usually pasta. I needed time to decide. I hesitated to ask the stewardess what type of beer they had because for some reason I couldn't say the word "beer" without sounding like a complete idiot. It always came out as bear, bare, or bare. Mind you, they were complete idiots for not figuring it out. Why in God's name would I be asking them what kind of bears they had on board? Just a white wine with the chicken for me. I could finally sit back, enjoy my food, and get pissed. They say you get drunker faster because of the air pressure or something. I couldn't care less about the science behind it, I just needed it to help me forget how cramped I was. The next obstacle was eating. That was the one time I wished I was in business class. Not only because the food was better, but have you ever tried eating a meal with a plastic spork while your elbows were touching? Go ahead. Try it. I counted down the hours and kept checking the flight information screen to see how much more torture I would have to take. We were finally making our approach to Charlotte, North

Carolina. I lifted the window cover, put the seat in the upright position, and then started searching for my shoes.

I always wondered why they were so adamant about making sure all the seats were in an upright position. I doubt that a quarter inch recline would really be the thing that saved my life in the event of a crash landing. I'm no rule breaker, though. I got myself ready to land. Being on the window side did mean that I was at the mercy of the person on the aisle. I hoped she was one of those people in a rush to stand up, but she was still engrossed in her book. I had a connecting flight to catch, so I wanted out. The queuing continued the second the engine was switched off.

From the outside, it looked like any other airport, but I have to say the inside was heavenly bright. I joined the painfully long queue at passport control and tried my best not to look suspicious. I had nothing to hide, but the presence of law enforcement always made me nervous. I was cutting it close. My connecting flight to Nashville was in seventy-one minutes and I had just seen a sign beside me that read '60 minutes from this point'. I still had to pick up and drop off my bag, go through security, and trek to my gate. I tried to raise my concern with the queue manager, but he said there was nothing he could do, and that other people had connections too so he couldn't put me in front of them. They should have a separate line for people with connecting flights, and it should be organised by time. Time flies when you're in a rush, and border control officers definitely slow down.

I finally passed the grilling, bags, and security, with less than two minutes to find and get to my gate before it closed. I was that guy running through the airport to catch a plane. People started walking slower, as if they wanted to show off how much time they had. It was out of my control. I blamed the airline for scheduling the flight with such a short gap in between. I finally locked eyes on the gate, which, of course was on the other side of the airport, and saw that nobody was there. I wasn't surprised, just disappointed. It wasn't the end of the world, but it was still extremely annoying. I looked up at the screen and for the first time was thankful, "delayed," by an hour. Relieved I hadn't missed it after all, bothered that I had run for nothing, but mostly delighted I had time for a drink. There was a sports bar conveniently located right opposite the gate. I sat down, caught a breath, and ordered a pint of Stella. Just as I was about to order my third, I saw a couple of people starting to gather, so I quickly settled the bill and walked straight onto the plane. No queue.

5

Arriving at the plane, I could see why. It's hard to have a queue of five people. It was the smallest plane I had ever been on. I had to duck to get in. That was the last time I would be able to stand up straight. There was no first class. To the left was the cockpit, and to the right were maybe fifteen seats, if that. It was like a plane for children. The seats did look slightly more comfortable, though. Nashville must not have been that popular of a destination, I guessed. There was no doubt I was sitting next to an American chap. He was wearing a bright coloured Hawaiian shirt, shorts, white socks and trainers, but the biggest giveaway was how happy he looked. He had started a conversation with me before I had even sat down. "Where you off to?" he asked. Same place he was, I hoped, but I politely specified that I would be staying in

Franklin. Within five minutes, I knew everything about the gent. I knew that he had three kids, one was a doctor, the other was travelling in Europe, and his youngest, Emma, was a vet, who had just opened her own clinic. He and his wife, who was sitting in the aisle seat opposite him, had just returned from a cruise that they went on for their 25th wedding anniversary. I knew more than even his doctor needed to know. The only time he stopped talking was when the pilot came on the speaker. I don't know why. The plane was so small we could all see him standing right there. He proceeded to tell us that he was going to take it up to a cruising altitude of 25,000 feet then bring it down to 18,000… He was going through all his moves. I was sitting there thinking why he was telling us. I didn't care how he was going to do it; I just wanted him to get us to where it said on the ticket in one piece. We didn't update him on what I was going to do throughout the flight. I was going to sit there for a bit, then I might eat some peanuts, and then if I was lucky, take a little nap. The stewardess did her pointing dance and showed us how to use a seatbelt. I was so glad that they explained I had to lift the metal buckle to open it because otherwise I would have chewed my way through the fabric. I mean, if you're not smart enough to operate a seatbelt, you shouldn't be allowed to fly. I was surprised they didn't instruct us how to release the tray table. They always request that you pay close attention to the safety information even if you have flown before, as some things might be different. To this day, it has never been any different. Life jackets were reportedly under our seat, but has anyone actually ever checked? Has anyone in the history of these announcements reached down, pulled it out, checked it for holes, made sure the little light on the shoulder is working, and tested the whistle? No. We were just supposed to take their word for it. With all the cuts, I wouldn't have been surprised if there was nothing down there. In case of a drop in pressure, oxygen masks would fall from the overhead panel. They were strict on that you put yours on before helping anyone else. That's the one time they want you to be selfish.

Brian Hudson, the guy sitting next to me, continued with his life story. He was born in Michigan, but moved down to Jackson, Tennessee many many years ago. He worked in commercial real estate, but has since retired. The stewardess walked by handing out bags of pretzels. The plane was too small for trolleys; she was just pulling them out of a carrier bag. I was pretty full, but my free stuff radar was on full blast. Soon after, the pilot started his descent, and before I knew it, we had touched down in Nashville town, thirty minutes ahead of schedule.

It wasn't like Heathrow where you would have to go into a holding pattern for an hour while they made space for you to land and then you would have to waste another hour taxiing on the ground looking for a gate to park. We landed straight at the gate, the seatbelt sign was turned off a few seconds later, and within the space of less than five minutes, we were disembarking. Stepping into Nashville airport felt like stepping back in time. The carpeted terminal was filled with fifty shades of brown. Passengers were queuing to get on the plane we had just gotten off of. I was tired and dreading the queues, but there was none of that. No passport control, no customs, no nothing. It was like getting off of a bus. It came as a nice surprise that domestic flights within the US were so relaxed. It being so huge, you forget that it's still one country.

The next thing that shocked me was that the baggage claim was in the arrivals hall. Anyone off the street could have walked in, picked up a bag and walked off. Strange. Even in Dubai, where they chopped off the hands of thieves, they kept the baggage claim in a restricted area for ticket holders only. There was always that feeling of extreme anxiety while I waited for my bag, hoping that they hadn't lost it. Seeing that there were only a handful of people at the airport, my suitcase arrived pretty quickly. I lifted it off the carousel and followed the signs to the taxi rank. The whole experience was painless.

There were a few yellow cabs parked up with the drivers huddled close by having a chat. They were almost surprised that I approached them. I threw out the word "Franklin?" in that general direction. One of the chaps said he would be happy to take me, but that it would cost me $50. I quickly did the maths in my head. It was only around £30, so I agreed. He then did something I had never witnessed a taxi driver to do. He turned down good business, to save me, the customer, money. He advised that at that time of night the shuttle bus was most likely empty and that they could take me for closer to $30. Wow! In London, hungry taxi drivers went out of their way to screw you, but these guys went out of their way to help you. I was loving Tennessee. I almost wanted to pay extra to reward him, but I took his advice. I walked over to the large blue shuttle van. There was a shifty looking man with a painter's brush moustache. I never trusted men with moustaches. We only had to reference history for that one. To be fair, I never trusted women with moustaches either. Before I could even tell him where I was going, he grabbed my bag, shoved it in the back, and got in the van. I tried sliding the door open, but he rolled down the window and told me to get in up front.

He was driving like he was in a rush, but I hadn't even told him where we were going. I wondered where he would have taken me if I didn't speak up and tell him that I wanted to go to Franklin. He nodded, continued the route he was going down, and without much confidence said that we would find it. What did he mean we'd find it? We couldn't just drive around and hope we'd eventually end up there. I didn't know there was a 'we'. I was sure taxis worked on the principal that 'he' would find it and take 'me' wherever I wanted to go. Like the pilot, he started telling me the route he was going to take. I had never been to Tennessee before so he could have been talking French. He did let me know that there was no traffic on the roads that night so it wouldn't take us more than twenty minutes. Brilliant. I was more than ready to retire. It was only around 8 p.m. local time, but it was in the middle of the night for me. It felt a lot hotter, and humid, than London, but because it was so much more south, it was already dark. The one and only benefit of British summers was that sometimes it wouldn't get dark until 10 p.m. I looked out of the window, to see nothing. We were driving fast down a derelict country road. There wasn't another car in sight. That was when my thoughts started getting the better of me. Was he in cahoots with the taxi driver, and was actually taking me into a forest to have his way with me and then kill me? It would have been the perfect setting for it. I had never seen it, but I couldn't stop thinking of *The Texas Chain Saw Massacre*. I started making a mental note of everything about him and everything in the van in case I needed to tell the police later. Who was I kidding? I wouldn't have been able to get away. "So, where you from?" he asked in a thick Southern accent. That just made him scarier. All he needed was some dungarees and a shotgun.

I regretted telling him I was from London. He

continued the conversation asking what brought me out to Tennessee and if it was my first time. I should have told him I was there to see friends and that I had been several times before. Honesty isn't always the best policy. I was the perfect target for him. We sat in silence, but he kept looking over at me. After an awkward few minutes, he asked me what church I belonged to. What sort of a question was that? There was no way I could answer that in a way that would save me. He didn't find it funny when I replied, "All of them." At the height of my paranoia, he steered the conversation from religion to guns. Great. He was a gun enthusiast. He told me that in Tennessee most people had a carry permit and that he was always armed. Shit! Shit! Shit! Just then, he slowed down and started looking out of the window. It was extremely dark, so I was sure he was looking for an appropriate place to dump my body. He asked me to check if I could see any of the house numbers on the mailboxes on my side. 1479 Mapleberry Drive. Phew! I made it. He offered to help me with my bag, but I told him I would manage. As I started walking away, he rolled down the window and called me back. I hesitantly returned to the car and saw that he was writing something down on a piece of paper. A receipt? He wrote down his name and number and invited me to his church followed by a barbecue at his house with his wife and family the next day. He even offered to pick me up if I needed a lift. Mr. Psycho moustache serial killer turned out to be a really nice guy. I felt bad for thinking that he was going to bury me in the woods. I had no intention whatsoever to actually go, but it was a sweet offer.

For some reason, I was expecting the Wild West, but the neighbourhood was a lot greener. Well, black because there was no light, but I could sense the grass. As I approached the house, the security light came on, illuminating the quaintest little cottage. An American flag was flying proud like it was an embassy. There was a beautiful front porch complete with two antique-looking white wooden rocking chairs, a comfy porch swing, and dozens of flowerpots. I searched under the welcome mat for the key, but couldn't find it. I started panicking. I looked under every single one of the plant pots, to no success. I lifted the mat up again, completely, but still nothing. I tried the door, but it was locked. I sat down on one of the creaky rocking chairs to think. There was no way to contact the owner of the house so late at night, and I was in the middle of nowhere. I checked the number a few times on the door 1479 before realising I was at the wrong house completely. I was supposed to be at 1497. Doh! I quickly walked away from the house, worried that the people living there might have thought I was trying to break in.

Luckily, I wasn't too far off and located the right address. It looked almost identical. If possible, even cuter. I walked up to the red door, and just as instructed, found the key under the welcome mat. The house was beautiful. Dark wooden floors, bright walls, and lots of interesting things to look at. It screamed character. The decor might have been a bit grandma-ish with all the little knick-knacks, but it was clean and added to the charm. My feet were exhausted, so the first thing I did was take my shoes off. I put my suitcase to the side and took a little tour. It was a lot bigger than it looked from the outside. The kitchen was fully stocked, and the lady I had rented the place from was kind enough to fill the fridge with essentials. She had even left a postcard on the table welcoming me to Tennessee. I could get used to the Southern hospitality. I unpacked my Yorkshire tea, rinsed out a dusty china mug and let the kettle boil as I continued opening all the doors. As soon as I found the master bedroom, I collapsed on the squeaky bed. As I lay there, I could hear the crickets chirping away outside. A sound so familiar that I had never heard before.

I woke up the next morning at 5 a.m. not knowing where I was. I used to enjoy that curious feeling, but it kind of frightened me. The excitement of being there, mixed in with the jet lag forced me to spring out of bed. I drew back the curtains to see what my surroundings looked like by day. The sun was just starting to rise, but

I could tell it was going to be a lovely day. The cup with the tea bag was still on the kitchen counter, so I reboiled the kettle and made myself a nice mornin' cuppa. I discovered a plate of blueberry muffins on the kitchen counter that I had somehow missed. That settled breakfast. I was eager to explore the town and start the day, but it was too early. I decided to kill some time by switching on the TV. After all, that was what Americans were famous for. I found a show called *Duck Dynasty*. I liked ducks. After the first episode, I was hooked. Four hours later, only when the mini marathon had ended, I got ready, put my shoes on, and head out. It must have been around 11 a.m. I didn't know anyone and hadn't done much, well any, research on what there was to do. I turned my phone off and left it in my suitcase. The decision was mostly down to the fact that I didn't want to pay the extortionate roaming charges, but I also thought it would be more of an adventure that way. No safety crutch. Just the world and me. I wanted to be free. I made it a tech-free vacation. Detox.

6

Chris was still interested but was starting to fidget, waiting for me to get to the point. I had to wait my whole life so he could wait a little longer. I ordered him another beer, and myself another whiskey and continued...

Eddie King

7

I stepped out of the house and stood there for a moment to take it all in. It was the perfect little street. The houses were small, but all had white picket fences surrounding extremely well kept lawns. There I was thinking us Brits were the gardeners. The only noticeable difference was how each house had customised their mailbox. I started walking down the street towards the main road that I came in on the night before, not knowing exactly where I was going. The plan was to stumble upon a local pub where I could get lunch. I finally got to the main road. I say main road, but there was really nothing there. I looked left, nothing, right, nothing. I took the left. I must have walked at least an hour when I started wishing I had taken the right. I was at the point of no return, and was enjoying the stroll, so I continued. I was bound to hit something, if not the state border. Every thirty minutes or so, a truck would speed past. It was easily another two hours until I saw a little cluster of buildings. There was a solicitor's office, a bank, a tanning salon, a dry cleaner, and finally what looked like a sports bar. Everything was closed, but the parking lot was full. I looked across the road and saw a bright white building. I saw the light. It was Sunday, and everyone was at church.

I spotted a man leaning against his car in his church suit smoking a cigarette. I walked up to him and asked him if he knew of a restaurant or pub nearby that I could get some lunch. He knew the area well and must have spent twenty minutes going through all of my available options. He gave me a lot more information than I needed but told me that the closest place that would be open was a bar back in the direction I came from. Great. Surprisingly I wasn't too tired, so started my long trek back. It seemed faster but took longer. I eventually got back to my house and carried on walking. It was starting to get dark, well dim. Literally five minutes along, I came to another little cluster of buildings. I really should have taken the right. There was a café, a Mexican restaurant, a cupcake shop, and right there on the corner a large neon sign, Losers Most Wanted Sports Bar and Grille. The "L" was a six-foot tall cowboy boot. I don't know how I missed it. Yep, it was this very bar. To this day, I find the name genius. Not much has changed. I walked in, sat down on a stool at the bar and was greeted by a barmaid very much like this one. The only thing that changes is their names. I had missed lunch, so I just ordered a pint. She, Britney, kindly went through the beers they had on tap. I didn't recognise a single one on the list. That was a dead giveaway that I was from out of town, out of the country. Like today, it wasn't very busy, so we got to talking. She told me how it was her dream to travel around Europe, especially London. She had just graduated from UTK and was bartending until she could find a job. I can't remember what exactly she majored in, but it was one of those useless ones that didn't lead into a career. It was a good thing she knew how to pull a pint and interact with the customers. She told me that on a good night she could make up to a thousand dollars on tips. She was cute. She ticked all the boxes, blonde hair pulled up in a ponytail, blue eyes, tanned skin, a tight body, but for some reason I wasn't physically attracted to her. It's not always an exact formula. She was extremely friendly though, and the only reason I stayed there for another three drinks. She let me sample all the beers, but there wasn't a single one on tap that tasted good. They did have Stella in a bottle, so I just stuck to that.

I thought she was just being extremely friendly because she worked for tips. What happened next proved that she was genuinely nice. It was around 7 p.m. She said she was clocking off early that evening because her friend was having people over at her house for drinks and that if I didn't have plans that I should stop by. I didn't have plans that whole month, and didn't know anyone, so of course I accepted. She wrote down the address on a napkin before she ran off. I waited for her to leave, downed my drink, and rushed home to get ready. I had walked close to six hours that day, so thought I probably ought to take a shower and put on a clean shirt for the party. As soon as I got home and took off my shoes, I contemplated bailing and staying home to watch more *Duck Dynasty*. The jet leg and beer were making a pretty convincing case, but it was an opportunity I couldn't miss. An opportunity I shouldn't have missed. Plus, if that was my local, I'd be seeing Britney again, and didn't want it to be awkward. She was kind enough to invite me, so I had to fight through. I put on my best khaki trousers, a pair of nice brown suede loafers, and ironed a dress shirt. They were all slightly different shades of light blue, so it wasn't too hard to decide which one.

I called for a taxi, and when I told the driver the address of the house in the neighbouring town of Brentwood that I was going to, he seemed very impressed. I realised I should take a bottle of wine, so I asked him to stop at a grocery store along the way. He took me to a place called Walmart. They didn't have them in London, but I had still heard of it, and knew that I could get anything and everything anyone ever needed from there. I told the driver to keep the metre running, and that I was just going to run in, pick something up, and would be back in a minute. I walked in and was absolutely flabbergasted. I had never seen anything like it. It wasn't a grocery store; it was a grocery city. It was the biggest building I had ever been in, and all on one floor. It went on for miles in every direction. It was so bright and colourful, I wanted to stop at every aisle, but I was already running late. I was definitely going to go back and spend a whole day there. Many of the customers looked like they did. They were like zombies with trolleys. I walked the entire length of the store and finally reached the drinks section right at the end. I hoped the driver was still waiting. I thought a nice bottle of red wine would be suitable. Soft drinks, beer, so much beer, every type of beer, even some I recognised, but I couldn't see any wine. I searched and searched, but no wine. I thought maybe they had a separate section closer to the tills because I didn't see any spirits either. I walked all the way down to the front again, but didn't come across it.

I asked one of the tired cashiers where the wine was. She shocked me when she told me that they didn't sell wine or spirits. How could a store that sold everything, not have the most important thing? Apparently it was a law that supermarkets couldn't sell wine or spirits. But they could sell beer? That made no sense to me. Jesus drank wine. I thought we were supposed to be in the Bible Belt. She quietly whispered that there was a liquor store right next door where I could get some. It was like she was sending me to a back alley to buy drugs. That made it seem even more ridiculous. I told the taxi driver I'd just be another minute, and ran to the place, hilariously named Frugal MacDoogal. I picked the most expensive Italian red they had, which was still quite reasonable, and hurried back to the car. It was already nearly 10 p.m. so I found myself in a bit of a rush. Luckily it was only ten minutes away.

The cab pulled up outside the most beautiful white mansion. It was ginormous, like one of those Southern plantation palaces. It had large pillars that fronted a deep double-decker porch. The lawn was impeccable, striped like a football pitch. I walked up the long drive, which was lined with cars. I saw that as a sign that I was in the right place. There was a note on the door reading, "We're in the back," with an arrow pointing to the left. I followed the path around, admiring the wrap around porch. It made mine look like a plank of wood attached to the front. There were signposts with arrows leading me to the back, in case one would get lost. It was pretty dark, but distant laughter over light music, assured me that I was going the right way. I started getting nervous. I didn't know what I would do when I saw the group. I thought I should just ask for Britney, but what if she looked different, or I didn't recognise her and I asked Britney for Britney. I was always rubbish at recognising people. Was her name even Britney? I started doubting myself. Maybe her name was Tiffany. I thought if it were Britney, I would have made the connection with Ms. Spears, but I hadn't up until that point. I was starting to panic. As soon as I turned the corner, I was welcomed with a big cheer. I had a feeling they did that to everyone that joined. Britney, definitely Britney, ran over, and gave me a big hug.

She was holding one of those red solo cups. Up until then, I had only seen them in American college movies. We didn't have them in London, so it had become a symbol of American parties. She announced me to the group and told them all I was from England. That was the most exciting thing about me. My USP, I guess. I was greeted with another drunken cheer. There were maybe fifteen people dotted around a fire. A couple of people sitting on chairs, a couple on a log, but most of them were cross-legged on the ground. Britney returned to the circle, leaving me standing there. Three strumming guitars would every now and then break into a song that everyone else knew the words to, but I had never heard before in my life. I didn't want to sit on the ground and get my trousers dirty, so I hovered around awkwardly for a bit. I was expecting something completely different and was definitely overdressed. Everyone else was in shorts, t-shirts, and flip-flops. I even hesitated wearing flip-flops on the beach. Everyone seemed to be engrossed in their own conversations and all knew each other very well.

8

I could hear a note being picked on a guitar coming from outside the circle. I saw a girl sitting on the tailgate of an oversized red Chevrolet pickup. The truck was old and dirty. There was no shine left to the paint, but it was better than sitting on the floor. It was backed up close enough to the circle to hear the conversation, but far enough from the light of the fire that I couldn't make out enough. I trotted in closer to investigate, still holding the neck of the bottle of wine I had brought. I was instantly drawn to her burgundy cowboy boots swinging by the Tennessee licence plate. I slowly tilted up her photoshopped tanned legs. It was exactly like those scenes you get in movies when they introduce the sexy girl character. She was wearing short blue cut-off jeans and a white stringy top. Long blonde wavy hair, that looked like it had just been styled for a Hollywood red carpet. She picked a string or two and then recorded it down in her notebook.

She knew I was standing there, but didn't acknowledge me. In my smoothest British accent, I asked if she minded if I sat down. She looked up, premiering big bright blue eyes that reflected the moonlight. "Yes." Did she mean, "yes, I do mind," or, "yes, please sit down?" She lifted her notebook from beside her and shuffled over to the left. I leaned up on the edge of the truck, with my feet firmly on the ground. I introduced myself, but it seemed like she already knew who I was. Brit had told her she met me at the bar and invited me. What else did she tell her? I thought.

"My name is Madison. Never Maddie. Always Madison." She had a sweet bubbly voice with a slight twang and talked real slow.

I held up the bottle of wine as an offering but told her I didn't have any glasses. She put her guitar down, jumped off the truck, and told me to wait right there. I hoped I didn't scare her off.

A few moments later, she returned with a couple of those red solo cups. I had never drunk a fifty-dollar wine from a plastic cup before. It almost felt wrong, but still tasted great. I probably should have given the wine to the host or at least Britney, but I was happier drinking it with Madison. She repeated everything I said in an attempted British accent. She loved the way it sounded but wasn't very good at replicating it. It was cute. Failing, she concluded that English people talked funny. I wittily responded that it was "Eng-lish" we were talking, putting extra emphasis on the "Eng."

"Yeah, but we are in Amer-ica," she quipped back, humorously putting the emphasis on "Amer."

"Mad-ison."

She had a beautiful, warm smile. The more I talked to her, the more I discovered, the more I wanted to explore. I don't know how we got on to the subject, but we started talking about space. We tried to fathom the size of the universe and our place in it, which led to whether we were alone in it. It was one of those things I liked to think about, but never took the time to. She created that moment, and knew a lot about the planets and stars. She was fascinating. There was a genuine optimism and positive outlook to the world, which started shining through me. She made me believe that everything was just fine and dandy. At that moment, everything was. We raised our plastic cups and downed the wine. She picked up her guitar, strummed a few chords, whispered something under her breath, and then quickly scribbled it down in her notebook. I tried to peek at what she was writing, but she pulled it away so that I couldn't see. She wasn't shy or embarrassed, just extremely humble. Her face lit up like she had just solved in impossible equation. It was clear she was doing something she absolutely loved, and that just made her even more attractive.

I asked her how long she had been writing songs for. All her life. Her parents moved to Tennessee when she was just 4-years-old. Her father was an entertainment lawyer, so he had some connections in the industry. She was working on getting a few songs ready for an EP that she could shop around to a few of the big music execs. She slammed the book closed, hopped off the truck, and put the guitar in the back seat. I was surprised to find out that it was her truck. I pictured her in a bright sunflower yellow VW Beatle.

"Nice car," I sarcastically, but politely stated. It actually was quite nice. Her mum's Jeep was in the shop, so she was driving her Mini, leaving her with *Old Betsy*. I stepped back to take another look. London was packed with characterless Ferraris and Lamborghinis, but you'd never see a vehicle with so much charm and story.

She slammed the tailgate shut. "Wanna go for a drive?" she offered.

"Sure!"

She climbed up to the driver's seat, leaned over and opened the passenger door for me from the inside. It only opened from the inside. It was just as roomy as it looked. She had feminised it with feathers, fluffs, and an Indian dreamcatcher hanging from the rear view mirror.

The engine sounded like the complete

opposite of a Prius, and you could feel it was working hard. I should have told Britney I was heading off, but Madison zoomed out of the drive and down a pitch-black country road. Large imposing trees lined the side of the street, shading any light. All I could see were two freshly painted solid yellow lines separating the straight lanes as far as the headlights reached. She turned the radio up loud and sang every word in tune. That was the first time I had heard cookie-cutter country, but I liked it. All the songs were about her. "With her long blonde hair, pretty little eyes so blue, a little shy side, a little wild side, in some cut-off jeans, ain't nothing in the whole wide world like a Southern Girl," indeed.

9

I had no idea where we were going apart from that it was her favourite place. I really hoped it wasn't a nightclub. A few miles down the road, without breaking speed, she jerked the car to the right. I thought she was trying to dodge a deer or had lost control. It got very bumpy, very fast. I held on to the side rail for dear life and tensed my legs, but there was absolutely no change on her. She continued singing, which meant she had either completely lost the plot, or she knew exactly what she was doing. I really hoped it was the latter.

If it was possible, it became even darker. There was nothing in sight, but vast nothingness. She finally slowed down and yanked out the key from the ignition, which brought the truck to a rolling stop. Shit, I thought maybe she was the one who was going to pull out a shotgun and bury me in the woods. They do say it's the ones you least expect. Don't they? Why did I think everyone in Tennessee was going to kill me and bury me in the woods? I guess because it was so easy to do. Nobody would know where to look for me, everyone carried a gun, and there were a million and one places to bury a body where the police wouldn't even think to look. I was the one starting to think like a crazy serial killer.

"We're here," she said. I looked around, confused. I was definitely missing something. "Her favourite place?" I questioned myself. I wanted to ask her why, but stayed silent. I tried to figure out where we were, but all I could make out was that we were in the middle of a field. She stepped out, slammed the rusty door behind her, and said that she was going to show me what the South was really about.

There was a touch of adventure, wildness, and thrill to her. I quickly unbuckled my seatbelt and followed her out. She popped the tailgate open, rolled out a blanket, and sat down inside cross-legged. I stood around for a moment, still not fully knowing what was going on. She told me to get in. I climbed up and sat with my back against the side facing her. My eyes were behaving oddly, so I blinked hard a few times to reset, but it didn't help. I started hallucinating small dots of yellow light, which would appear for a few seconds everywhere I looked and then disappear into thin air. I ignored it at first, but it persisted. I needed confirmation, so told Madison about it. She reached out, caught one of the lights in her hands, and brought it closer. I was glad she saw it too, but it really freaked me out. Lightning bugs. I hated bugs, but she assured me that they were harmless. Still, I didn't feel comfortable with the alien UFOs.

We sat there for ages, talking and getting to know each other more. I wanted to know everything. I liked to play the favourites game. Her favourite movie was *Aladdin*; mine was *The Shawshank Redemption*. My favourite food was Eggs Benedict; she liked sushi, but also loved a good catfish dinner. Her favourite animal was a toss-up between a dolphin and a butterfly, but when I chose dogs, she made me change it to a lion because she wanted all the dogs to herself. She wanted all the animals. She had a kind heart, big enough for everyone and everything. I didn't know exactly what a Southern Belle was, but I bet she was one. You could tell her parents brought her up right.

We shared our dreams. She had completed a year of Art History at Belmont University, but dropped out to chase her love for music. One day, she hoped to go on a big arena tour around the world. The idea of getting to see new countries and experience new cultures while doing what she loved. She felt the most comfortable when performing on stage. Not because she wanted to be the centre of attention, but because she could truly tell the world how she felt. I could never be in front of an audience. I couldn't even do karaoke. We were so different, liked different things, came from different worlds, had different dreams, but that just made our time so rousing. I had only met her, but it felt like we had known each other our whole lives.

"It's time," she whispered. She lay down flat facing up and pulled me down next to her to do the same. My lumbering legs were slightly too long, so I had to rest them up on the side. I turned my head to ask her what we were doing. She giggled and pointed straight up. It took my eyes a few moments to adjust, but then there it was. Wow! The more I looked, the more stars appeared. Before I knew it, the whole sky was decorated with sparkling diamonds. I had never seen anything quite like it.

There I was, lying next to the most beautiful girl I had ever imagined in the back of a truck in the middle of a dark field that went on for miles in each direction staring up at the stars. I reached over and grabbed her hand. A tingle shot through my whole body. Her skin was soft. She scooted closer, cuddled up to my arm, and leaned her head on my beating chest.

Neither of us wanted to be the one to bring the night to an end, but it was getting late and cold. We were in the middle of nowhere, so I really hoped she was going to drop me home, or somewhere I could get a taxi from. Madison suggested that we head back to her place because her parents weren't home so we could hang out more. I didn't object, secretly fist-pumping the air with joy.

We got back into the truck and she muscled her way back onto the country road. We didn't make it very far down the road when she complained that her steering was getting extremely heavy. I could feel the struggle. She pulled the wheel once hard to the right and killed the engine. She didn't know what was wrong, but I heard the wheel flapping, so suspected it was a flat tyre. We both got out to investigate and noticed that the front right tyre was punctured. Airless. Her frustration grew massively when she realised that she wasn't getting any reception. I mean, we were in Nowhere, America. I didn't have my phone with me. It was unlikely we would see another car until morning, so we were stuck.

I saw it as an opportunity. She had been the one in control the whole night, so it was my turn to steer the ship. She started to get worried. She had automatically dismissed my presence. It was time to restore order and remind her that I was the man. What better way than to do that than to save a damsel in distress. I had changed a tyre once, be it on my small Mercedes C-Class, but I was hoping the principal was the same. I calmed her down and told her to wait in the car while I sorted it out. She was more surprised than impressed, so it was vital I proved myself. I rolled up my sleeves and started my search for the spare. I looked everywhere. I found the jack tool in a little toolbox in the back, but there was no sign of a tyre. That's when I started to get worried. There was no boot and nothing that lifted up, so the only other place it could be was underneath the truck. I gave hope on protecting my beige trousers and committed myself to the ground. Jackpot. Well, I had located it, but the next step was to figure out how to release it. I struggled for a bit, untightening and tightening a number of bolts until it finally dropped out onto me. The jack looked a lot different than the one I had used before, but somehow, by the grace of God, I figured out which way around it went. I hoped, anyway. Madison jumped out to see what was going on and lend a hand, but I told her to just stand back. I had an audience, so I needed to smoothen my actions. The angels must have been with me that evening because I lifted the beast up, unscrewed the bolts, hammered the wheel off the axle, popped on the spare, tightened it up, and brought the whole thing level again, with not too much trouble. I cannot explain how macho I felt. I wanted to jump on the bonnet and beat my chest like King Kong. I did in my head. I had achieved something great. I stood there appreciating my handiwork when Madison came up behind me, put her hand on my shoulder, and patted her applause. After that, she was impressed. I had saved the day. My only concern was that it stayed on long enough to get us to civilisation.

On the drive back, she thanked me endlessly and genuinely felt bad that my clothes had been ruined in the process. Before I knew it, we were back at the house the party was at. I thought maybe she needed to pick up something or wanted to say goodnight to her friends. Most of the people had left, but there was a small group hanging out in, on, and around a newer and even bigger pickup truck. Madison flashed the headlights on full beam and pulled up beside them. It was Britney and a few others from earlier. She came to the window, gave Madison a big hug, and blew me a kiss goodbye. They all got into their truck and drove off.

Madison sped up the drive, clicked the garage door opener attached to her sun visor and parked up in a garage that was more spacious than the house I was staying in. Only then did I piece together that it was actually her house. I was admiring the clean garage. Everything was organised and packed away in large labelled storage cabinets. There were a couple of vintage motorcycles, a sports car hiding under a cover, a bunch of bicycles, and a foldaway table tennis table in the corner. I didn't really notice anything after that. I was still processing everything, so we sat there in silence for a moment. She reminded me that her parents were out of town for the week and invited me in to finish off the delicious bottle I brought. At least the wine went to its rightful owner, I thought.

"Where did they go?" I asked. Where? Where? What difference did that make? Who cared where they were? It was the only thing I could get out. I think even she was a little surprised by the question because she didn't answer it. Note to self, and every other man out there, if a beautiful girl invites you in, you don't ask any questions, you just say yes. She felt really bad that my clothes were all dusty and muddy so offered to give them a quick wash. It wasn't necessary, but I wasn't going to turn down hanging out with her longer. She struggled to get the key out of the ignition and jumped out.

I followed her into the house and was instantly blown away. It was impeccable. We went in through the sparkling white marble kitchen, to the subtly grand hallway. Dark hardwood floors, a simple, but very large chandelier, a couple of art nouveau pieces dotted around, and an iron spiral staircase right in the middle. It was both modern and traditional at the same time. I'm sure there's an arty word for that, but I'm not an interior designer. She told me to wait there and ran upstairs. I noticed framed photos hung up around the room. There were cute baby pictures of who I assumed was Madison, her graduation photo, her prom photo, her high school cheerleading squad photo. Yep, she was a cheerleader. What more could I ask for? There were tonnes, many with her family and friends. The picture of her, her parents, and their golden retriever looked like an advertisement for a holiday resort.

I started nosing around the other rooms. It was very open plan, so it wasn't like I was opening doors. I always loved seeing what the inside of other people's houses looked like. To see how others lived. There was a lot to look at, but it didn't seem cluttered. It was very tastefully done. How I would do my house one day.

The lounge was wide and deep. Large enough

for the grand piano not to look out of place. It was dark, but I spotted a lot of instruments, some on stands and some scribbled on and displayed on the walls. The only instruments I could play were the recorder and the triangle, but it was very hard to stand next to a piano and not press a key. Just as a couple of the high notes rung, Madison's glowing outline appeared in the doorway. The light from the hall behind her illuminated her long blonde hair. She looked like an angel. She had taken off her boots, and replaced her outfit with a long loose t-shirt, but somehow still looked like a million bucks. She was holding some folded items of clothing in her hand. She had pulled out some clean garments from her "daddy's" closet for me to wear, while she put mine in the wash. She was not going to let it go. My protest was cut short when she told me I wasn't supposed to be wearing shoes on the rug I was standing on. I looked down, shit, and quickly tip-toe-jumped back into the hall. I apologised profusely, but she just laughed it off. She handed me the clothes and pointed to a bathroom down the hall where I could change.

The guest bathroom was nice too; very spacious and equipped like a hotel with all the miniature toiletries and fresh towels. I didn't really feel comfortable wearing her dad's clothes. I could feel the situation was getting out of control. Was I supposed to wait at her house while she washed my clothes or was I supposed to go home and see her again the next day to make a swap? It seemed excessive, but it also meant that the worst outcome was either spending more time with her, or seeing her again. She knocked on the door and asked me how I was getting on. I replied with my final plea to call it off. I couldn't wear her dad's clothes, and the last thing I wanted to do was to remind her of him. She said that most of the things were things her dad had bought, but had never worn because they were too small, or too big, or not to his liking anymore. Great, I was going to look like a clown in the mismatched wardrobe. I actually liked one of the polo shirts, but none of the trousers fit me. I kept my dirty ones on but walked out in the new polo shirt. She was waiting right outside the bathroom door. "Are you wearing underwear?" she asked confidently.

"Yes?" I questioned, knowing exactly where she was going. She held out her hand and like a bossy mother ordered me to take them off. Feisty. I cheekily joked, "You could at least buy me dinner first." I unbuttoned and stepped out of the greasy trousers. They really did need a wash. I don't know how they got so dirty by just changing a tyre. It was more like I built a whole car in them and then rolled around in wet mud for thirty minutes.

She took my clothes to the laundry room by the kitchen, leaving me standing in her hallway in her dad's polo T-shirt and luckily my nice boxer shorts. Sexy. She called out to see if I was hungry and wanted some food. I declined out of politeness even though I was a little peckish. I could hear her loudly opening and closing drawers and cabinets in the kitchen. She reappeared holding the bottle of wine, two glasses, and a platter of cheese, crackers, and grapes. That's when I knew it was love. It was like she had read my mind.

Forget the fact that she was the most beautiful girl I had ever seen, or that she was a talented musician, or that she had cool friends, cool things, and that she lived in a modern day palace, she had a kind, caring heart, and that's what mattered most. I followed her upstairs to the first-floor lounge. It wasn't as fancy as the one downstairs, but more comfortable with large fluffy sofas, and a big screen TV. She put the wine and midnight snacks on the coffee table and collapsed on the couch. I gently sat down beside her and poured her a generous glass. We kept each other entertained with facts and stories from our past and continued talking about our desires and dreams for the future.

She put her glass down on a side table, and then grabbed mine out of my hands and carefully placed it next to hers. It didn't take me long to realise what her actions were saying. It had never been clearer. I leaned in ninety percent and met her supple red luscious lips. It was a short kiss, but the sensation lingered. They say a girl can tell everything from the first kiss, but I knew too. That one kiss changed, improved, my life forever. For me, that was both the beginning and the end. Nothing in the past mattered. I was totally indulged in making the present my future. I instantly became a believer in "the one." It was an indescribable feeling of joy and security. Everyone talked about it, many tell themselves they have felt it, but only a few are ever lucky enough to actually experience it. Those who deny it have been denied themselves.

Our noses and foreheads leaned against each other as we sat in anticipation. I gently pushed back her golden hair, placed my hand on the side of her neck, and kissed her again, harder. I cautiously ran my other hand down and lifted the back of her t-shirt to caress the small of her back, which was smoother than silk. She responded by throwing one of her legs over and straddled me. Remember, I was in my boxers, so you could only imagine the complications. My hand slowly crept higher up her side as the one from the back of her neck dropped to rub her upper thigh. It was happening. I went to lift off her top, but she straightened her arms down resisting. She managed to squeeze one word out at a time between heavy kisses. "Can't. Not. Here." For a moment, I was discouraged, until she grabbed my hand, and without breaking lips, led me down the hall to her bedroom.

Her room was a huge dimly lit pink cave. I didn't inspect the furnishings in detail because I couldn't take my eyes off of her. We kissed to the foot of her bed, almost tripping a few times. It was all happening very fast. She placed both her palms flat on my chest and then with one blow pushed me back onto the firm mattress. Again, she got on top of me. I tried leaning forward, but she pushed me back down flat. For a shy, quiet girl she was forceful. She leaned up straight and seductively took off her shirt, not breaking eye contact once. Like everything, to no surprise, her tanned body was flawless. She lunged back at me. I had never been with a girl I wanted more in my whole life, but there was no pressure. She made me feel at ease, so I could fully focus, and enjoy. It was my turn to take control. I grabbed her by the hips and rolled her over onto her back. I saw that she had a little butterfly tattoo on her side. I wasn't big into tattoos until that point. It was small, about the size of a tuppence, and suited her. It showed that there was a little wild side hidden underneath my Southern Belle. I'm not going to go into too much detail, but I will say that there was no trace where one was once two. We fell asleep cuddled up close, hand in hand.

The sun blared through the partially open blinds and bounced off the all-white bedding. It was like I had woken up in heaven. It took me a moment to recall the night before. It almost felt like a dream. I reached over to make sure it wasn't, but there was nothing but duvet. I dug my way out of the oversized, over-fluffy pillows, sat up, and got familiar with my new surroundings. I was definitely in her room, but she wasn't there. I spied a clock on her wall. It couldn't be noon. I thought the jet lag was supposed to wake me up at 5 a.m. again, but I guess we didn't go to sleep much earlier than that. I zombied my way out of bed and called out for Madison. I made a quick pit stop at the loo, shook hands with the old vicar, and made my way downstairs to find her. I followed my nose to the smell of bacon coming from the kitchen. For a moment, I hoped her parents hadn't come back and I wasn't about to meet them for the first time in their kitchen in my boxers. Fortunately, it was Madison. She was extremely awake bouncing around in yoga pants, a tight tank top, and trainers, with her hair tied back in a ponytail. Very sporty. How was it possible that she looked just as beautiful?

"Good morning," I croaked. She greeted me with my favourite, Eggs Benedict, but said she didn't have any ham left, so hoped I didn't mind that she substituted it with bacon. That was the nicest thing anyone had ever said to me. I couldn't believe it myself. She was becoming unrealistically, and dangerously perfect. She noticed me up-and-downing her sporty attire, so explained that she had spent forty-five minutes on the treadmill in the garage. It was an every-morning habit she had just gotten into and didn't want to break. She apologised that she didn't have time to change, but we both knew she looked cute in her workout clothes. Breakfast was complete with a big glass of freshly squeezed orange juice, a plate of cut fruit, cereals, milk, coffee, and toast. It was like a hotel buffet. I don't know whether it was because I was starving, or because she made them, but the Eggs Benedict were definitely in the top three I had ever had. It didn't take me long to wolf them down.

She went into the laundry room and came back with my clothes washed, dried, ironed and folded. I was sure she had a maid back there. I guessed that was her way of kicking me out. She said that she was going to jump in the shower in her room, and that I could use the one in the guest bathroom in the hall, or the one in her parent's room. I, of course, chose the guest bathroom. I always found it weird showering in other people's houses. I was ready pretty quickly, so I waited for her in the upstairs lounge. It took me some time to figure out how to turn on the television. It was always a lot harder than it should be. First you would have to figure out which control operated what. I tried looking for the *Duck Dynasty* show I was hooked on, but got caught on *FOX News*. The presenters all looked like Hollywood movie stars and models. Very different from the BBC anchors. I was sitting there for a while, but she eventually came out wearing a bright flowery sundress and her cowboy boots. As much as I didn't want to, it was time for me to get up and go back to my house. I asked if I could use her phone to order a taxi, but she refused. She thought it was understood that she would drop me home. I really didn't want to trouble her, but it did mean I got to spend more time with her. That's all I wanted from that point on... her time.

Eddie King

10

I admired my handiwork on the tyre again before getting in the truck. She said she really liked the neighbourhood I was staying in and had a lot of friends that lived nearby. It wasn't anywhere near as impressive as hers. The houses were unique, but shared common characteristics. They all sat atop beautifully kept lawns, with long winding driveways, and black iron gates. They all had black iron gates. The sun was shining high in the sky, the music turned up, windows down, sitting next to Madison. It was the life I never knew I wanted. It felt good. It felt right. We arrived at my house a lot sooner than I had hoped. We sat there for a while in silence. I really didn't want our time together to be over, so I suggested we go for a cup of tea at the café across the street. It was a long shot, and was preparing myself for an excuse, but she answered by switching off the engine. That's when I knew that she wasn't done either. It was very easy for her to have declined if she wanted to, but she didn't. She wanted to be there just as much as I wanted her there. I wanted her there always. We walked over to the café, a concept many Americans weren't familiar with. Walking, not cafés.

As we walked in, everyone's heads turned to look at us. I was so proud to be standing next to her. We sat across from each other at a booth by the window. It was an artsy little place, an independent Starbucks kind of deal with a hint of 1950s diner. A waitress came over and poured Madison coffee from the jug she was carrying around. She was about to pour me some, but I covered my cup and asked for a cup of tea. "Sweetened or unsweetened?" I had never been presented with those options before.

"Umm, just a normal cup of tea please."

"Sweet or unsweetened?" Asking the same question twice wasn't going to change my answer. Madison helped and said it was ice tea.

"No, just a regular cup of hot tea. English breakfast or Earl Grey would do."

The waitress looked at me strangely and then said that she'd go and check if they had any. You would have thought I was asking for caviar at McDonald's. She came back a few minutes later with the milkiest, weakest cuppa I had ever had. I took a few sips, thinking of the real tea I had back at the house. Madison picked up one of those *Nashville Scene/What's on in Nashville* magazines left on the table next to us and started asking me how much of the city I had seen.

Well, seeing as I had only been there for a couple of days and wasn't really the tourist type, not much. She insisted that we did a day of all the sites. The Country Music Hall of Fame, Grand Ole Opry, The Ryman Auditorium, Broadway. I thought Broadway was in New York. I wasn't much of a museum person, but I wasn't going to turn down a single second spent with her. I would have spent eternity in hell if she was by my side because she made me feel like I was in heaven. She was dog-earing the pages of things we could do, propping up at the idea of going honky-tonking. I had no idea what honky-tonking was, but it sounded a bit rude. It did sound more fun than a museum, though. She said we had better get going if we wanted to miss rush hour traffic. I thought she meant that we should do it someday, I didn't realise she wanted to go that day there and then. Her keenness was flattering. I didn't need much convincing, and it seemed like she had already made up her mind. I quickly paid the bill, left a tip way too generous for the liquid the waitress had served me, and left before she changed her mind.

It was only a twenty-minute drive to Downtown Nashville. Everything was always only twenty-minutes away. She was a good driver, but a little fast for my liking. I was hardly ever in a rush, and if I was, I always listened to the "better late than never" advice parents gave their children. She complained how expensive parking was, but to an Englishman that fell on deaf ears. If only she knew the extent to which we were being ripped off in London. We found a spot not too far, and walked towards Broadway and 2nd. It was a very strange strip, a bit of a hotchpotch. A few touristy gift shops, a couple of high-end restaurants, bars, clothing shops, and offices. I know that was what you'd expect from a high street, but nothing seemed to fit together. There was no flow. The tired neon signs failed to brighten up the dated street.

I grabbed Madison's hand as she explained the whole culture and customs of honky-tonking. The closest thing I could link it to was a pub-crawl if pubs had loud, live country music blaring out of their doors.

We walked past a bunch of drum solos and came to a place called *Tootsies Orchid Lounge*. Madison told me that all the country legends used to frequent *Tootsies* once upon a time and that we had to go and check it out. We found a table near the back on the ground floor, apparently there were four or five floors with different bands playing different styles of country music on different stages. The band near the entrance played all the classic country covers. Everyone on the street loved a little Johnny Cash and Elvis. The band was actually quite good. There were a few faceless guys plucking and drumming away as the lead lady belted out those powerful lyrics. She was hittin' it. At one point, she even got on the bar and started dancing *Coyote Ugly* style. A few of the tourists around us were up there with her in spirit, but boy was she feeling it. She took those songs to a whole new level. It was too loud to talk, so we just sat back, had a few drinks, and enjoyed the show.

The plan was to hit a few places along the Nash Vegas strip, but we were too comfortable at *Tootsies*. Madison came over and sat on my lap. I wrapped my arms around her from behind and held her tight. I didn't ever want to let her go. Time flew. It wasn't until the kitchen closed that we realised we had missed dinner. We stepped out to what felt like silence. Most of the restaurants were closed, but Madison had a flash of brilliance and hurried us back to the car. She didn't tell me where we were going, saying that she wanted to keep it a surprise, but really also feared that her explanation wouldn't do the place justice and I wouldn't want to go.

She pulled in to a place called Sonic. It looked like a mix between a drive through McDonald's and a petrol station. I opened my door to get out, but she stopped me. She rolled down her window and asked me what I wanted. I squinted at the menu and asked for her recommendation. She ordered us a couple of bacon cheeseburgers, some chilli cheese fries, and a Blue Mountain Berry Blast slushy drink. There were tables outside, but we sat down on the tailgate. A few minutes later, a futuristic fast food employee roller-skated over to deliver our meal. That totally blew my mind. It was exactly the sort of thing I wanted to do in America. Fancy restaurants are the same in every city, but that was something I had never seen before. The food was delicious too. Ridiculously unhealthy, but absolutely scrumptious. I understood why America had an obesity problem. I unconsciously yawned. "Am I boring you," she jokingly called me out. Not at all. The jet lag was kicking in. She switched on the engine and offered to drive me home. Again, I didn't want the night to end. We had come close to calling it a few times since we met, but always managed to figure out a way to keep it going. When I was with her, I felt like nothing could bring me down. She made me feel like the best version of myself. She made me the guy I wanted to be. That's how I knew I had a keeper.

You'd think after twenty-four hours together she'd be sick of me. There was definitely a sense of sadness on the ride back. She pulled up outside my house. We must have sat there idling and chatting away for at least an hour. It was so easy to speak to her. We reviewed the day's events, and I thanked her for being my tour guide. I thought I'd try my luck one more time, and invited her in for a cup of tea. I was sure she'd want to go back to her house, but if you don't ask, you don't get. I enticed her in with the real Yorkshire Tea I had brought from London and was absolutely thrilled that she accepted.

She thought the house was wonderfully cute and found it hilarious that a grown man was staying in such an old granny's house. I put the kettle on the stove and gave her the not so grand tour. It was large by London standards, but tiny compared to her palace. I know it wasn't mine, and I was just renting it, but I was slightly embarrassed by it. At least it was bigger than a hotel room, I told myself. She took off her boots and got comfortable on the couch. As soon as I took my load off, the kettle started whistling. The kitchen and dining room were open plan, so I told her to turn on the telly and check for *Duck Dynasty*. I made the tea in a china pot I found in one of the kitchen cabinets. It looked like it had never been used before, but was sure the lady I was renting the house from wouldn't mind. I put together a plate of biscuits and served her in a sterling silver tray. Only the best for the Queen of the South. As hoped, and maybe also slightly expected, she said it was the best, most flavourful cup of tea she had ever tasted. I took full credit as if I had picked the leaves myself. It was getting to that crucial time of the night again where decisions had to be made. I really wanted her to stay, so I took full charge. I put my tea on the ironic coffee table, instructed her to do the same, and without any hesitation, boldly went in for the kiss. Those who hesitate… She said she had been waiting all day for me to do that and was starting to get worried that I didn't like her. I overruled being a gentleman and took care of business right there on the couch in the living room.

11

Chris holds up his glass to cheers me. "Nice one." Out of courtesy I clink, but remind him to be careful because that was my wife we were talking about. I break his fear with a smile. I notice that Ashley has been less involved in her phone and has her ears sitting with us. She brings us another round of drinks, and instead of going back to her station, sticks around, leans forward, puts her elbows on the bar, palms on her cheek, and waits for me to continue with the story.

12

Madison rummaged through my closet, found a t-shirt, and wore it as a night-dress. It was all she was wearing, but damn did she rock the hell out of that look. That was her speciality. She looked fabulous in anything and everything. It might have been the late boost of caffeine, but we weren't sleepy. It was too hot to get under the covers, so we lay on top, holding hands, talking. I didn't want to just know everything about her, I wanted to know her. I wanted her to know me. I didn't keep anything from her. I usually only focussed on the good bits, but she made me feel so comfortable that I shared everything with her and she shared everything with me. Everything we were going through in our lives, we were from that point going through together. We were each other's therapists. Both of my parents had passed away from illness and old age a month

112 Eddie King

apart from each other two years prior. I was an only child, didn't have much family, none that I liked enough to stay in touch with anyway. I was alone in the world and was at that scary point where I really needed to figure out what I was going to do with my life. She sympathised and told me that she went to college for a year but had dropped out to focus on her music career. A huge, and maybe unwise risk, but she was always one to follow her heart. Her parents were always busy and flying all over the country, so she was left to make and face the big scary decisions alone. I comforted her and told her she made the right one.

The topic of age, one that I wasn't looking forward to, eventually came up. I feared that I was maybe a few years too old for her. Up until then, we didn't know exactly how much of a gap there was, but we knew there was one. She had barely left her teens behind and I was knocking on the doors of the next decade. She had achieved a lot and was mature for her age. I wasn't, so we met in our mid-twenties. It wasn't that big of a gap, really. I didn't feel it, and I was just hoping she didn't either. Our mental age was the same, so that's all that mattered. We talked about everything, even things you weren't supposed to on a first date, if you could still call it that. We had still been going on from the night before, and I hoped we continued to do so. There were things we disagreed on, sure, but we were able to respect each other's opinion. That's not to say we didn't have our fair share of debates. Things I changed her mind on, and things she opened mine to. We had found the perfect position, so for the rest of the night, only our lips moved. The room gradually became brighter. We had been up all night. It was as if we were making up for lost time. Surprisingly, we weren't sleepy at all. I sprung up and filled the kettle. She took the duvet around her shoulders and went to sit on the porch swing outside. I brought it out to her and cosied up under the quilt. I controlled the light rocking of the swing with my feet. We sat there in silence watching the day come in. She put her cup down on the floor, leaned her head on my shoulder, and fell asleep.

We spent the rest of my week there together every day. I wanted to stay in with her, and we did some days, but she made sure I got to see everything the city had to offer. She even managed to drag me on a historic tour of Franklin, which was actually quite fascinating. What I found the most fascinating though was the names of the shops, restaurants and cafés we went to. *The Puffy Muffin*, *Frothy Monkey*, *Piggly Wiggly*. Every night, I encountered much anxiety to the possibility of having to go our separate ways, but somehow we always found a way. From the moment we had met on that tailgate at her house party, to my last day in Tennessee, we had been together. We were practically living together. Sometimes at her house when she needed a change of clothes, and sometimes at mine. We even stayed at a hotel Downtown one night because we got too drunk and didn't want to drive home. The time was filled with laughter and happiness. We were so high that for a brief second we forgot the fact that it couldn't last forever. I would eventually have to return home to London. That didn't stop us from making plans though. We fantasised about holidays that we wanted to take. She was a lot more adventurous than me, but she did manage to sell me Bali, Fiji and a few others. We talked about things we wanted to do, films we wanted to see, and sports we wanted to play. She made everything feel like it was possible. We even booked concerts we both wanted to attend. Before the trip, I didn't know much about the new generation of country music, but Luke Bryan sang the soundtrack of my time with Madison.

Our time did finally come to an end, however. I wished that the sun would forget to rise because I knew the morning would bring bad news. I was punched back into reality. Thousands of miles were preparing to separate us. Anything further than by her side was too far for me. We both knew it was coming, but it came too soon. I packed my suitcase in sombre silence that morning. She offered to drive me to the airport, but I thought it would be better if we said our goodbye in private. I didn't want my last memory of her to be surrounded by strangers. What else was there to say? We didn't know when the next time would be. If she lived in France, it wouldn't have even been an hour on the train, but she was a whole day away.

The taxi pulled up outside and honked the horn. I opened the door and signalled that I would be two minutes. I handed Madison the key and told her to leave it under the mat before she left. I gave her a long tight hug. Emotions were high. She tried to control herself but broke down in tears. In a week, we had gone from being complete strangers living our very different lives in very different parts of the world to not being able to live without each other. I held her close and assured her that we would be together again. I was trying to assure myself that too. The taxi driver honked again. I peeled off and loaded myself into the cab. Madison stood in the doorway wiping her tears away and waving. Just as the driver pulled off, I ordered him to stop. I swung open the door, ran up to Madison, held her head in my hands, and passionately kissed her. I made her a promise that no matter what it took, I would see her again soon. I felt sick saying goodbye to her. There was a lump in my throat and I started violently coughing. I got in the taxi and tried to gather myself. The taxi driver checked to see if I was okay through the rear-view mirror and offered me some water from his bottle flask. It was a kind offer, but I didn't know where that bottle had been. We arrived at the airport.

Everything seemed slower and a lot more difficult than usual. The smallest inconveniences vexed me. I was in a bad mood, and I knew exactly why. Anger had absorbed my sadness, which was only made worse by airport processes. It was already a long, tiring flight, so you can only imagine how internally frustrated I became. I was feeling horrible, like I was going to be sick. Everything hurt and I was having a hard time with the cough I had picked up. One of the air stewardesses squatted down beside my seat and asked me if everything was okay. Nothing was okay. I told her that I was just sad to be leaving. I was uncomfortable, I had already seen all the movies, and the Jack Daniel's and Paracetamol cocktail wasn't working. At least the tailwind was on my side. Just as I was getting excited to be landing an hour sooner than expected, the pilot announced that Heathrow was extremely busy so we would have to enter a holding pattern until we were cleared for landing. Great. After forty minutes, we finally started heading down only to realise there was no parking. We didn't have a gate assignment, so we had to taxi around for an additional forty minutes. It's ridiculous. One of the World's busiest airports should have dozens of runways and terminals. London was even greyer than I had left it. I finally got off the plane, passport control, baggage claim, customs, taxi, and home. I was in a daze. On top of all that, it was, of course, raining and I didn't have a brolly. It wasn't that poetic rain that represented hurt, just pathetic constant drizzle.

Eddie King

13

I was struggling to drag my suitcase up the three flights of stairs to my apartment. I had no energy. As soon as I got in, I let my suitcase drop to the floor. I went straight to change into my white towel robe, which I had lifted from a hotel I once stayed at. I grabbed a beer, and assumed the fetal position on my sofa. I saw a post-it note stuck to my television remote. I tried reading it without moving but was forced to temporarily free my arm to pick it up. It was from Will, informing me that he was up North in Newcastle to pick up his daughter, Ally, and that they'd be back on Wednesday. I let the note drop to the ground, closed my eyes, and fell asleep before I could even take a sip of my beer. My dreams were just reruns of my time with Madison. I would drift in and out of the nightmare that was my reality. It was like that for the next few days.

My only movement was to answer the door for the pizza man and to go to the loo. That really was it. I was in a real funk. Life just didn't seem worth it without Madison. I felt like I had to punish myself for not being with her and definitely didn't deserve any pleasure or normality without her. My days were defined by daytime pizza and night-time pizza. The same order for both. A side of chicken strips, medium stuffed crust pepperoni, six sour cream and chive dips, and a 500ml bottle of Coke.

The few hours that I wasn't asleep, I was watching Animal Planet. I found a new appreciation for wildlife. Big cats were my favourite, but sometimes I was forced to go deep into the ocean. The doorbell shocked me up. It got to a point where I didn't even remember ordering the pizza anymore. I got to the door and saw that it was slightly open. I pushed it closed, undid the chain, and swung it open to see Will standing there holding the key up like a sword, "I return thee." I turned around and shuffled back to the sofa as he complained about the door chain. He followed me in. He commented on the leaning tower of pizza boxes on the floor next to the sofa and then my unsightly appearance. He never was one to hold back and didn't care whether he was being rude or not. I think maybe that's why we never extended our friendship outside my apartment and the communal hall we shared. I wasn't saying much, so he started. He apologised for not being around the last couple of days, explaining that he drove all the way up to Newcastle to pick up his daughter, but her whore of a mother, also known as his stunning ex-wife, didn't let her come back with him because he was half a day late. I could tell he was upset, and wanted to talk, but I was already maxed out with my own problems, which were more important. To me, anyway.

The doorbell rang again, breaking his rant. I let him answer it because I had used up all my energy on letting him in. It was the pizza man. Will returned with a slice already in his hand. I didn't mind, I wasn't that hungry anyway. I just ordered it for the sake of it being lunchtime. He helped himself to another slice, opened one of the dips, took a bite, and pressed again. He stood and pulled up the blinds to get some sunlight in. I held my hand up to my face like a vampire protecting himself from the poison daylight. He expressed great concern that it was in the middle of the afternoon, I was in my pyjamas, I had pizza boxes stacked up, I hadn't shaved in days, and that I also needed a shower.

His first question was who broke my heart. Nobody. I fell in love. He was quick to respond that if that was what I looked like when I was in love, something was definitely wrong. Something was wrong. Everything was wrong. I told him all about Madison. I wanted to tell everyone, but I had nothing to show for it. He was surprisingly sympathetic. He listened intently but was confused as to why I was acting like she had broken up with me. I didn't have an exact answer myself, but it just felt right, because life without Madison wasn't a life. He polished off the pizza and started cleaning up. He moved the boxes near the door, threw out the empty bottle of Coke, tidied up the table, fixed the sofa cushions, cracked open a window, and tried to snap me out of it. He insisted that I shave, shower, put on some clothes, and join him for drinks with his friends at the pub around the corner. I really didn't want to leave the house, but he was extremely forceful. I never took Will to be a wise man, but he did help me realise that instead of being sad that Madison and I were apart, I should be happy that I found the girl of my dreams and focus on ways of being with her again. I was occupied with the wrong emotion. There was happiness there, I just needed to bring it to the forefront. Still, I couldn't be bothered to go out, even though I could see the local from my window. If Madison wasn't there, it just didn't seem worth it. What could I have possibly gained otherwise? My apatite was starting to come back, and Will had hoovered everything up. I could have just called for another pizza, but I didn't want the delivery guy to judge me.

So, I went for one drink and some hearty bangers and mash. That's one thing America didn't have. I sat on the side and tried keeping to myself. Will did his very best to drag me into all the meaningless conversations. Pub talk. When I wasn't talking about Madison, I was thinking about her. I was becoming that guy. It wasn't very cool. Will's friends were friendly enough, but I looked around and felt like I was in a completely different story. I had been to that pub a thousand times, had walked the streets my whole life, and had been surrounded by those same people, well, not those exact same people, but the same breed of people, but all of a sudden it all felt alien to me. It was more than just holiday blues. My heart was in Tennessee. It was like taking a character from one of those sunny American rom-coms and sticking them in *Lock, Stock and Two Smoking Barrels*. Okay, maybe that wasn't the best example, but you catch my drift. I stayed the appropriate amount of time, and then hurried back home. Baby steps. As much as I didn't like to admit it, leaving my house did me good. It gave me clarity. I knew what I had to do. I had to figure out a way to see her again.

Sounded easy enough, right?

I was going to call her but thought it would be more romantic to send her a handwritten letter. I sat at my big leather top mahogany desk, pulled out the nicest paper I could find from one of the drawers, and opened the fancy ink and pen set I had once bought myself for Christmas, but never got around to actually using. I dipped the pen in the burgundy ink, and started writing, "Dearest Madison, words can't des-." Shit, I should have written *can not* or *cannot*. It would have sounded better than *can't*. I scrunched up the paper, tossed it in the direction of the bin, and tried again. "To my dearest Madison," I thought maybe that sounded too much. I scrunched, tossed, and started again. "Madison," yeah, I liked that. It was informal, but loving. I continued, "Words cannot describe." Sounded a bit cliché, and if words couldn't describe how I felt, then why in God's name was I writing her a letter. I needed something more original and something truer. Scrunch, toss, try again. Either I spelt something wrong, the ink smudged on the page, or it wasn't straight, but there must have been fifty little scrunched up pieces of paper around the bin, and I think one or two that actually made it in. I finally wrote one eloquent enough for the medium. It just didn't feel right to write *lol* in ink. It was bad enough that I used it in the digital sphere.

I told her that I had arrived back home to London safely, how much I missed her, thanked her for the most magnificent time, and that I was devising a plan for our reunion. I sealed the envelope with wax and stamped in my initials. Sealed with love. Writing the letter really made me feel better. For a brief moment it felt as if I was talking to her. We just had to take it one step at a time. Either I had to go back to Tennessee to see her, she had to come to London, or we met somewhere in the middle. My mind was racing as I contemplated with optimism because all three avenues led to me being with her again. That was the first night I had a good solid night's sleep. I woke up extra early that morning, excited to send her my letter. For once, I actually looked forward to going to the post office. I sent it special delivery next day signed for. I wanted to make sure she received it because too many times had I sent something and then sat around in suspense. It was a forgotten, and slightly nostalgic, process.

Handwriting a thought down on a piece of paper, putting it inside another piece of paper with a little door on it, walking it to a run down building where you had to wait in a long queue of angry people to talk to the rudest, most miserable member of society, who'd ask you to put the envelope on a scale, and then request that you hand over the most random amount of pennies in exchange for a tiny piece of paper with perforated edges, which you would have to lick and neatly stick in the top right-hand corner. Then you'd have to take the whole thing to a stumpy red cylindrical box and navigate it through the tiniest slot where it would sit until they collected it. Once they had picked it up, they would decide whether or not to put it on the right plane. Meanwhile, you would return home, refresh your browser a dozen times to make sure it had been scanned at the correct port, and when it finally reached the right country, it went to another post office in a town near to where you had sent it. Someone who hadn't gone to college would sort through the pile and hand it to a middle-aged man in shorts carrying a large bag who would eventually go and put it in a small box at the bottom of the driveway of the neighbour of the person you sent it to. Still, not bad for 37p.

I could have just sent her an email, but there was something special about receiving a letter. Surprisingly, it was delivered to her in the time they said it would. The next step was to anxiously wait for her reply. It was romantic, like we were characters in an epic romance novel. I waited for the postman every morning. A whole week had passed, and I was slowly starting to lose my mind. Had she not liked the letter? Had she forgotten about me? Had she moved on? I was weak. I gave in and sent her a text asking whether she had received my letter. As soon as I sent it, Will knocked on my door. He came in holding up a letter addressed to me that they had put in his mailbox accidentally. If only he had brought it in a minute sooner, I wouldn't have sent her the needy message. I tore it open and sat down to read it. She missed me too! It was a sweet letter. It wasn't as classically written as mine, but there were tons of x's and o's.

I spent the next few days devising the perfect plan. I had to take many things into consideration and concluded that I was going to fly her out to London. She had her time of being the one in control and with the home advantage, but it was finally my turn. I composed another letter attaching a plane ticket for her to come and visit me for a week. Well, it wasn't a real ticket because I couldn't actually book it without her passport number et cetera, but I mocked up a piece of card to look like one. Things like that only worked in the movies. In real life it was always more difficult, and not so straightforward. Plus, I didn't want to ruin the surprise, and had to confirm the exact dates that she would be free to come, so I would book once she had accepted. What if she didn't accept, though? There was concern that it was maybe too fast or too forward. A lot of thought went into it, so I took the risk. I needed a big gesture to keep her interested from thousands of miles away. I went through the whole process of sending the letter and again sat in anticipation for her reply.

One day, two days, three days, nothing. I was starting to get worried that maybe she took it wrongly or I offended her. My offer came from a good place, and I hoped she would see it that way. I sat around waiting for eight whole days before she replied. She was so excited and couldn't believe that I was going to send her a ticket. I would have sent her a whole plane if that was what it took. Metaphorically, of course, a whole plane would have been slightly out of my budget. We wrote back and forth a few times planning her trip. There was so much I wanted to show her, but we only had a week. We could sit by the river, or if the weather was nice, take a day trip to Brighton, or Bournemouth. She couldn't wait. I couldn't wait.

The day had finally come. I sprung out of bed and put on my best outfit. I had booked us a hotel, so I didn't have to worry about cleaning up too much. We could have stayed at my apartment, but I really wanted her to get the full London experience, which was in part, fancy hotels. I got the fanciest of them all. I didn't want her already very limited time to be wasted underground on the tube or stuck in traffic. I got one right in the centre of London. Mayfair. One of the dark blue properties on the Monopoly board. In fact, the hotel was on Park Lane, the other dark blue property. I had my C-class cleaned inside and out that morning on the way to the airport. It was luxurious enough that it was respected, but not so flashy that it would attract an audience like the bodacious supercars that paraded up and down Sloane Street all summer.

It was raining that morning, so I allowed

myself extra time to get to the airport. There was some added traffic, but I still got to the airport super early. I didn't mind though because it was a fantastic place to people watch. I found myself a comfortable spot near the front where I had a good view of both the flight information screen and the arrivals door. I was standing around for a good hour or two watching people connect. I was starting to get nervous. Not that she wasn't coming, but to see her again. Maybe nervous was the wrong word. It was more excitement mixed in with anticipation. I had missed her so much.

The doors swung open a final time. The whole of Heathrow lit up as she glided down the catwalk in slow motion with her hair lifted by the gust of the doors closing behind her. Her red suitcase obediently followed behind her. Tiny white shorts, a tight Victoria's Secret Pink hoodie, flip flops, and giant sunglasses propped up on her head. Comfortable, but somehow still chic. I could sense all the people around me staring at her, wondering which lucky fella she was there to meet. I felt so proud that it was me.

The bored taxi drivers erected their signs, hoping that she was their fare. I didn't call her name straight away, taking enjoyment in observing her as an outsider. As soon as she spotted me, she let grip of her suitcase, ran over, and gave me the biggest hug. Just like that, all my nervousness slipped away. Her kiss breathed life into me. Instantly, I felt great.

No word of a lie, as soon as we left the airport, the rain stopped and the sun came out. It was sunnier than it had been all summer. I didn't have a big red truck, but her large suitcase still fit comfortably in the boot. She noted that the truck wouldn't have even fit into the tiny little parking spaces. Another thing she pointed out was that everyone had reversed into the parking bays, but in America everyone would drive in and reverse out. That said a lot about the people. Americans took the easy way out, the reward first, and worried about the problem later. Us Brits took the pain first, so that we could enjoy later. I was smug in my explanation, but she argued that it made more sense, especially at airports and supermarkets, for the boot to be facing outward, so that it was easy to load. Good point, well made. We set out.

I told her I had booked us a hotel, but I didn't tell her which one because I wanted it to be a surprise. She managed to get some sleep on the plane, which was good because it meant that she fully rested, awake, and ready to go. She was so excited to see London. It was her first time in England. In fact, it was her first time outside of the United States. Apart from the one weekend she went up to Toronto, Canada for a wedding with her parents, but that was when she was 4-years-old, so it didn't really count.

I gave her a running commentary of landmarks along the way. Most of it was motorways and A-roads, so there wasn't much to tell, but when we got closer in, we drove past the Natural History Museum, the V&A, the Science Museum, Harrods. I assured her that we would definitely go to that last one. We continued towards Hyde Park and came to Wellington Arch. I was born, and lived in

London my whole life, but that was the only bit of history I knew. There to commemorate the Duke of Wellington and his victory over Napoleon in the Battle of Waterloo. It was important to know at least one fact. She was impressed. She loved history. She was intelligent and had a real thirst for knowledge.

Her head turned constantly as she decided where to look. There was too much for her to take in, and she wanted it all. Such places of interest were few and far between where she was from. I had driven up and down Park Lane thousands and thousands of times, but it was only until she pointed it out that I realised how green it was. There were random art sculptures dotted around that I had never noticed before. We looped right, then left, and pulled up outside the Dorchester Hotel. My favourite place in London. The doormen, in their top hats and plush green coat tails, welcomed us in. I handed one of them the key and told him that there was luggage in the boot to be brought up to the room. She admired the Rolls-Royces and Lamborghinis lined up. We walked up the couple of steps and through the revolving doors. She pulled on my arm and said that she felt way too underdressed for such a classy establishment. I put her at ease by explaining that it just meant that she was so important that she didn't have to dress up. The real VIPs in clubs were the ones that didn't have to put on shoes or a dress shirt. If they were in there in their pyjamas, then the club must have really wanted them there.

Truth was, she looked better than everyone there anyway. She had never been to such a posh place before. Large marble pillars bordered the most decadent, but elegant lobby. Madison wandered, taking it all in, getting caught by the shiny jewellery displayed by the lift. When making the reservation, I had told the hotel I was planning on proposing to my girlfriend. That way we'd get extra special treatment and maybe even a free upgrade. The friendly lady at the counter was quick to check us in and gave us the key to room 209. Note, it wasn't a key card, it was an actual electronic key made out of plastic that you would enter into the lock. It's all about the small touches. On the way up to the room, I showed off the Promenade, the bar I used to frequent. She was in awe. It was actually quite cute how excited she was about everything.

We opened the door to a spacious Executive Deluxe King Room. It was flowery with mahogany wood furniture. Lots of muted greens, browns, and deep reds. Earth tones. The pièce de résistance was the inviting four-poster centrepiece. She collapsed on the bed while I explored the rest of the room. I had stayed there before, a couple of times actually, but still felt compelled to open every door to see if there were any surprises hiding in the cupboards or drawers. I surveyed the bright white Italian marble art deco bathroom. As I bent down to check the brand of the miniature bottles of shampoo, Madison came up behind me and wrapped her arms around tight. She didn't have to say anything. I turned around and took her in my arms. We must have stood there holding each other in the bathroom for a good ten minutes. It would have been longer, but we were disturbed by a knock on the door. Must have been the porter with our bags I thought.

I was delighted to open the door to a bottle of Laurent Perrier champagne in a bucket of ice and a tray of Thorntons chocolate strawberries. The room service attendant hoped that we would accept the complimentary welcome treat from the hotel, carefully popped open the bottle, poured a couple of flutes, and wished us a pleasant stay. Madison raised her glass and thanked me. I was the one who should have been thanking her. I wanted to thank her every morning and every night for being her and choosing me.

I knew she liked sushi, so I made dinner reservations at my favourite Japanese restaurant. London was great for many things, but as you can tell, being a bit of a foodie, I was most eager to take her to all the amazing restaurants it had to offer. I had curated a secret guide of London hotspots. I wanted to show her my London. We nearly got through the bottle of champagne while she caught me up on all what was going on back in Nashville. There was another knock on the door. More champagne, I hoped, but it was our bags. She unpacked and started getting ready for dinner. She wanted to shower, do her hair and put on a nice dress. I thought she looked fabulous in those short shorts, but she had gone shopping for dresses, shoes, and bags before she came because she had heard how fashionable girls in London dressed, so she was dying to get all done up. The girls in Europe did dress on designer trend, but they had nothing on Southern style.

She disappeared off into the bathroom to start getting ready. I picked out a packet of peanut M&M's from the mini bar, lied down on the bed, and turned on *Top Gear* while she got ready in the bathroom. She was in there for quite a while, nearly two whole episodes. I called out a couple of times to see if she was alright and to let her know it was almost dinner time. When she did finally step out of the bathroom, my heart nearly stopped. In fact, I'm pretty sure it did for a few seconds. My chin was resting on the floor and my eyes were attracted to her like magnets. She was red carpet ready. Sparkly strappy stilettos tipped her long smooth tan legs, a short plain turquoise dress hugged her in all the right places, and I don't know what she did with her hair, but it was shiny and wavy like she was in a magazine ad for a hair product. It was wow. She tilted her head, hair flowing to one side, fiddled in some dangly earrings as she asked me if what she was wearing was appropriate. I was speechless. She asked me again, but I couldn't get a word out. My silence made her concerned. She tried once more, threatening to change into something more conservative, but I yelled out "No!" She sought confirmation that it was okay. I nodded my head like a hypnotised fool. I brushed off the M&M's that had missed my mouth and landed on my shirt, stood in front of her, ran my fingertips down her arm, and kissed her shiny red lips. She pulled back, worried that her lipstick had smudged. She used her finger to wipe off what had rubbed on to me. I tried enticing her towards the bed. Forget going out for dinner, we could just order room service. She didn't get all dolled up to stay in.

She stopped at the mirror unhappy that something was missing from her outfit. I wasn't going to get a better chance. I instructed her to wait there by the mirror. I went into my bag in the closet and pulled out a little red box. I had bought her a white gold and diamond Cartier necklace. I spent a long time in the Sloane Street store deciding between a heart and a cross pendant but finally went with the cross. I mean, she was from the Bible Belt after all, and it might have been hard to tell from the dress she was wearing, but she was a good Christian girl. I also feared whether it was too soon to give it to her, or if it was a bit much, but I couldn't wait anymore. Her eyes lit up as I handed her the box. A Hollywood actress couldn't have replicated her reaction.

Not worrying about her lipstick, she jumped on me to show her appreciation. Not enough to skip dinner though. I took the chain from her hand to help her put it on. I stood behind her as she lifted her golden hair. I gently stroked the nape of her neck and hooked the tiny clasp with my giant fingers. I could see her about to tear up in the mirror as she placed her hand over the cross hanging low on her décolletage.

We made our way downstairs and walked through the lobby. Holding her hand made me feel as tall as one could be. She was probably so used to people staring; she didn't notice everyone's eyes on her. We walked out of the front doors and strolled around deep into Mayfair. I considered a taxi, but she said she'd rather walk because the weather was nice and she could get to see London up close. It was things like the road signs, the architecture of the buildings, the layout of the houses, the cars, the smells, and the sounds that really gave her a true sense of the city. We walked through Grosvenor Square, home of the American Embassy ironically enough, finally arriving at a tiny door hidden away in a back alley. The best places usually were.

There was a steep, narrow staircase down to an authentic underground Japanese cave. Not many people knew about it, which was one of the things that made it so cool. I wasn't a huge fan of sushi, but I used to love that place. Nori San, the head chef, was always there preparing the most delicious delights in the teppanyaki style restaurant. Everything on the menu sounded so delicious, it took us quite long to decide. We ended up ordering a lot more food then we could eat. Madison exclaimed that it was by far the best sushi she had ever had and that they didn't have anything like that in Nashville. I was off to a good start. One for one. We sat at our table for hours just chatting away. Like we always did. She always kept me entertained with a funny story about one of her friends or something that happened to her. It was getting late, but she was still full of energy. I was full of sake, so was getting a bit tired. It was only her first night, so I didn't want to overdo it. It was hard because I was dying to take her everywhere and show her everything. She wasn't used to wearing heels, so we took a taxi back to the hotel, and settled in for a drink in the Promenade. Marco, the bar manager, who knew his regulars well, seated us at my favourite table. I ordered my usual Jack Daniel's Old Fashioned and a passion fruit martini for the lady. Every girl I had ever known loved that drink, and it came in an impressive glass. She did love it. That was two for two.

We did all the museums, galleries, and touristy stuff during the day. We managed to cram in quite a lot. I talked her out of the London Eye, but we went up to the top of The Shard, visited the Houses of Parliament, the Tower of London, and Buckingham Palace. It was the nights I enjoyed the most, though. That was when I could show her the London she wouldn't find in her tour book. I had built up the necessary relationships at all the exclusive restaurants, bars, and nightclubs, so each night we dined at restaurants like Nobu, Alain Ducasse, Gordon Ramsay's, The Ivy, and Le Gavroche before drinking the night away at a swanky cocktail bar.

I was devastated that it was our last full day together. We wanted to make the most of the day, so we woke up early and took a lovely stroll through Hyde Park. It was a little chilly, but the sun was out. Rich yellow, red, and brown leaves blanketed the path. We made our way to Harrods. She was mesmerised by the whole concept and couldn't believe how much people would pay for such gaudy items, but she also wanted to buy everything she saw. We walked around for a few hours testing out all the perfumes, picking out furniture, she tried on loads of expensive shoes on the fifth-floor shoe heaven, while I painted my dream behind the perfect barbecue. We picked up a couple of sandwiches, snacks, and wine from the food hall, and a colourful selection of macaroons from Ladurée. We walked back towards Hyde Park and found a spot overlooking the Serpentine Lake. We were that typically annoying, young loved up couple in the park. We sat cuddled up keeping each other warm all afternoon. All of a sudden, out of nowhere, I started coughing violently again. The last time was in Tennessee on my way to the airport, but it had been fine since then. She asked whether I had gone to the doctor, but it was only a cough. She wanted me to promise that I'd go get it checked out, but I just brushed it off. I knew my body better than any doctor, and knew it would be fine. She seemed concerned, but I was more concerned that we only had sixteen hours left together.

We slowly made our way back to the hotel, which was only across the road, to get ready for dinner. We were all fine dined out, so that night we went to celebrity pizza joint Ciro's on Beauchamp Place in Knightsbridge. I knew the owner Ciro quite well, and the manager, Alex, would always treat my party and me to free shots. I once sat next to Prince Harry there, and you couldn't get a better endorsement than that. We followed dinner with a quick drink at a bar called Nozomi across the road before heading to Bouji nightclub. Tuesday nights were the busiest, but I knew Oliver, the owner, and he was kind enough to hook us up with a table in the VIP section.

I got to show Madison off to some of my
friends, more acquaintances, and she got to
experience a true nightclub. It was her first time.
They didn't really have nightclubs, as London
knew them, in Nashville, or Tennessee, or many
states for that matter. Even if they did, she
wouldn't have been allowed in because she was
only 20-years-old and the drinking age in the US
was 21. In Spain, it was 16. Oliver summoned
over one of the bartenders and whispered
something in her ear. A few minutes later, she
returned with a jeroboam of Dom Pérignon
champagne with a fiery sparkler on top.
Madison cupped her hands over her wide
mouth. I owed Ollie for that one.

She tried to get me up to dance with her a few
times, but I sat back and enjoyed the view.
Usually, when I used to go out in London, I was
in and out within twenty minutes, but we were
there till the lights came on. Neither of us wanted
to leave because that would mean our last night
together had come to an end. I wasn't going to

let that happen. I waved down a taxi and told him to take us to VQ on Fulham Road. It must have been around 4 a.m. but the restaurant was open twenty-four hours. We washed down our food with even more champagne. It was clear from our expressions that we were both thinking the same thing, but neither of us could bring ourselves to ask how we were going to make it work. Nashville was too far for me to go regularly, and London was too far for her. They say love always finds a way, but love wasn't thinking practically. We had to say bye, not knowing when, and even if, we would see each other again.

14

Ashley genuinely looked mournful. She fetched Chris and me another drink and poured herself one too. "Was that it? Did you ever see her again?" she asked. A part of me feared that I wouldn't. Especially with what happened next...

15

We got back to the hotel early in the morning, not giving her much time to pack. I offered to take her to the airport, but it was her turn to savour her last memory of me at The Dorchester rather than the airport. Using my own words against me. She gave me a lasting kiss, and then just like that, she was gone. There were still a few hours before I had to check out, so I thought I'd try and get some sleep.

My heart was racing fast and beating hard. I couldn't take the roller coaster ride of her coming and going out of my life. I wondered if long distant relationships actually ever worked, for normal people. I knew celebrities did it, but even they had trouble. I couldn't fly out to Nashville every weekend. I really didn't know what we were going to do. I wasn't getting any sleep, so I got up and ordered some breakfast to the room.

I went into the bathroom to brush my teeth but caught myself staring into the mirror trying to figure out what I was going to do. How and when was I going to see her? Again, I got into a coughing fit. I was convinced it was stress related because it always seemed to happen when I thought of Madison leaving or not being there. It was worse than it had ever been. I coughed and coughed and coughed until I spit blood out in the sink. The sight of blood freaked me out, so I thought it was time to call the doctor. The soonest appointment my GP had available wasn't for a few weeks. I thought by then it would get better, so let it be. I had my eggs, painfully checked out of the hotel, and returned home back to reality.

16

Days passed slowly. I was excited to receive a letter from Madison letting me know that she had arrived home safe and was missing London. She clarified that by London, she mostly meant me. That was all I needed to hear. I loved the fact that she had restarted our traditional correspondence. It just made each communication that much more special. A few exchanges in, and I knew I had to make my way back to Nashville. I planned to rent out my apartment in London for three months to go and be with her. I would have gone for longer, but that was the longest the government wanted me there. It was better than nothing, and it was all I could do. We would worry about the next stage when we came to it. I told you love would find a way.

The excitement of planning my visit got me

through the excruciatingly long days, but I was struggling at night. I would feel drained, deflated, and weak. It was getting worse and worse, eventually taking over my days. It all just deteriorated so fast. Will came over one evening to find me on the floor curled up in pain. I tried telling him I was okay, and that it was probably just food poisoning, but he called an ambulance anyway. I didn't have enough energy to get off the floor. Bless Will, he stuck by me, gave me water and leaned my back up against the couch. An hour had past, and there was no sign of the ambulance. I wasn't getting any better, drifting in and out of sleep. He called back a few times, but they said they were extremely busy and couldn't give an estimate of when they could get to me. Will offered to drive me to the hospital himself. I felt half dead, and knew something was wrong, so didn't put up too much of an argument. He put my arm around his shoulder, and lifted me up.

He shoved me in his tiny red Vauxhall and rushed me to the hospital. If there were ever a place that needed valet parking, you'd think a hospital would be it. In America, they have valet parking at the damn I-Hop. Circling around for thirty minutes looking for parking could have finished one off. Will didn't care. He pulled up in the red zone right outside the doors of A&E. He carried me in like I had been shot. I would have died before making the sort of fuss he did. It worked though because I got seen to straight away. With the aid of a nurse, he helped me onto a gurney in one of the rooms. I say room, it was more of a cubical. Three walls and a disposable paper curtain. I was stressing about Will's car a lot more than he was and told him to go and move it before they towed it away. He said he'd go park it and come back, but I insisted he go home. He'd already done more than enough. There was no reason for both of our nights to be ruined. I was surrounded by loud moans of pain. I could have joined in, but I had some self-control. I was almost embarrassed to make it a big deal. I was left there alone wondering if they had forgotten about me. I thought that if maybe

I yelled out a few cries of pain they might tend to me.

I was really uncomfortable. I hated hospitals because they were full of infections, diseases, and tropical illnesses. I don't know if it was the horror of being in a hospital, but I was starting to feel slightly better. It was always the case. Whenever I went to see a doctor, I always felt a lot better. It definitely wasn't because a pretty redheaded nurse in a tight white uniform was there to look after me. Nurses were like air stewardesses. There's a sexy image of them both etched in my head, but not once had I seen an attractive one. That was only in the movies. Well, some movies.

I didn't want to look silly, so when the nurse finally did come to check on me, I continued with my moans. I, of course, got the meanest looking one of them all in her oversized scrubs. Shallow, I know, but she wasn't competent either, so I wasn't going to spare her. She looked tired, overworked, and uninterested. Her attitude and tone proved that she was. She asked me to describe the pain I was having. What sort of answer did she expect? It hurt? Ouch? Bad enough to make me come to the hospital? She took a different approach and asked me to rate the pain I was experiencing. I tried to look at her clipboard to see if those were really the questions. Five stars? Very painful? First class? She clarified on a scale of one to ten with ten being the worst. I knew what she meant, I was just being difficult. At that moment I had dropped down to about a two, but if I said that she wouldn't have taken me seriously. I didn't want to go too high either, out of respect for the people that were there with their legs falling off, so I tried to explain to her exactly how I was feeling. She pressed for a number, so I gave her a seven. I searched for her reaction, but there wasn't one. I knew I should have gone with an eight.

She proceeded with the tests, rough in her movement. I always found the blood pressure machine fascinating. The one where they pumped air into an armband. If only all tests felt that nice. I detailed my symptoms and told her about the erratic coughing fits I'd been having. It was the first time I got her attention. She said she was going to pass on the information I had given her to one of the consultants who would come and see me. Panicked, she flagged down a doctor and handed him her clipboard. I couldn't hear what she was saying, but I knew it was something bad because he turned towards me and raised his eyebrows as she took him through the notes she had made.

He walked over and introduced himself as one of the duty doctors. He assured me that everything was okay, but that they wanted to do a couple of x-rays and take some blood just to be sure. Be sure of what? I worried. I let them get on with it. I was feeling better, so I knew it wasn't anything serious. Indigestion maybe. I sat in that miserable germ filled hall for over ten hours waiting for my results. I asked if I could just go home and come back the next day, but they had to keep me there for a reason they couldn't share. It wasn't as if they were doing anything. I was there so long, I saw the shift change. A different doctor came in, picked up the chart hanging by my feet and asked me the same questions I had been asked a dozen times all night. He informed me that some of the results weren't going to come in until the afternoon at earliest, so if I felt up to it, I could go home and they'd send my results to my GP. Why couldn't they have just said that at the beginning? I was frustrated that they kept me there for no reason but relieved that I could finally leave that death house. It was around 5 o'clock in the morning, so I got a taxi home and went straight to bed.

I only got a few hours sleep before my phone woke me up. It was the receptionist from my local surgery. I was surprised at their efficiency. I was sure they were calling to let me know I had picked up a nasty infection and that I'd have to go in to pick up a prescription for some antibiotics. She advised that I made an appointment with one of the *ology* departments at the hospital, as they wanted to run some further tests. There was no way in hell I was going back to that place, so I called up my health insurance company, and had them book me in at a clinic on Harley Street. I really didn't know what all the bother was. The worst of it was over. I thought I'd satisfy their curiosity, so I could continue planning my stay in Nashville.

17

The Central London clinic looked more like an office or hotel than a hospital from the outside. It was one of those white stone Victorian conversion buildings. Little hints of luxury like the gold plated handrails, wooden front doors, and a plant in the lobby made it feel a lot less clinical and, therefore, a lot less terrifying. The reception was intimate. Colours were soft and the lighting was dim. Large brown leather sofa chairs sat on a beige carpet. The staff looked professional and smart, dressed in suits. I had to make sure I was in the right place. A friendly Irish lady behind the desk took my name, told me to take a seat, and to help myself to some tea or coffee from the station in the corner, which I did. It kind of felt like I was back in school and was in the waiting room to go and see the head teacher. Not that my school was anywhere as nice as where I had found myself that afternoon.

I wouldn't say I was nervous, more intrigued to hear what they had to say. As nice as they had made the atmosphere, I still didn't like doctors. I had seen *House*. He could cure the most exotic diseases unknown to mankind, but he couldn't fix his damn leg. Always limping around. Or what about those two jokers from *Scrubs*? Were they really fit to practice medicine, and what was all this practicing business? I didn't want to be a guinea pig. I wanted them to have perfected medicine before they started treating me. All these humorous, but very real fears, played on my mind.

I didn't have time to finish my tea before the doctor called me in. He was a large man. Not overweight, but broad at the shoulders and narrow at the hip. Tall. Even taller than me. He was wearing a dark suit. Not tailored so that he looked like a lawyer or a city worker, but not cheap like a schoolteacher. He looked professional. There was something about him that demanded respect. He walked me down the hall to his huge office and sat me down at his desk. He was oddly friendly and instantly made me feel at ease. How a doctor should be. I felt safe in his presence. He asked me about my lifestyle, whether I smoked or drank. I may have exaggerated how much exercise I did and how little I drank, but I could honestly say I wasn't much of a smoker. The occasional cigarette, socially maybe.

He asked about the cough and how long I had been feeling unwell. Once I really thought about it, the cough had been lingering for a few months. It was more of a casual chat than the grilling I had received at A&E. The doctor, Dr. Stafford, told me about himself and his impressive qualifications. It was obvious he knew what he was talking about. He wasn't just book smart; he knew how to talk to people. He said he had looked at my test results, and from what I had told him about my symptoms, that in his professional opinion, he was sorry to say that it looked like, and then he hit me with it... cancer. What?! It was too harsh of a joke to make, so I hoped it was a bad dream. He had gone from being a lovely intelligent doctor to an evil liar, who obviously didn't know what he was talking about. He said we would need to do more tests, but that he had discussed it with another consultant and they both came to the same conclusion. I almost broke down. A million thoughts ran through my head, but Madison was at the forefront of all of them.

I was too young to have cancer. Cancer was what happened to other people. Cancer wasn't real. I told him he must have mixed up my results with someone else. I was just there for a nasty cold, or maybe the flu, at most. I couldn't have cancer. No one in my family had cancer. Maybe they diagnosed it wrong. Had they found a cure yet? Was I going to die? Was I going to lose my hair? How long did I have left? Would I need to wheel around an oxygen tank? I didn't know anything about cancer. I didn't want to know anything. He intercommed in one of the nurses and said that she'd show me to the main clinic where they would conduct some further tests. I thought I was just there for a consultation.

Lost in my own thoughts, I blankly followed the nurse through the long narrow corridors, down a sharp flight of stairs, through some double doors, up some stairs, through some more doors into what looked more like a hospital. There was a lot more white than the doctor's office, but still with small touches of luxury. They checked me into my own private room. The flat-screen TV, sofa, fridge, private bathroom with miniature toiletries, and a view of the gardens only distracted me for a few seconds. I quickly came back to realise why I was there. I nervously took a seat on the bed, not wanting to get too comfortable. A football team of nurses introduced themselves and proceeded with their appointed tests. It was all happening a little too fast for me to fully understand what was going on. I was feeling so uncomfortable, I wanted to tell everyone to stop and give me a second to myself, but, of course, I let them carry on without saying a word. I was rolled away for x-rays and scans and then pushed back for more blood and monitoring. They sent all the samples to their in-house lab and had the results fast tracked back to me within an hour.

I was lying there using the remote control to move the bed up and down trying to find a position. I was staring at the television, but I wasn't watching. All I could see was Madison at The Dorchester. The only thing keeping me from breaking down was that I knew, very soon, I would be on a plane to Tennessee to see my sweetheart. I was waiting for the doctor to come in and apologise for the mistake and say that it was an infection after all. There was a knock at the door. I tried to get myself decent, which was difficult in the hospital robe they put me in. Why the backside was open was beyond me and there was only one little string to hold everything together. They just made people look sicker than they actually were.

Dr. Stafford walked in and asked how I was doing. He wasn't wearing his blazer and had his sleeves rolled up going from room to room saving lives. He sat down at the end of the bed.

He asked if I had everything I needed, while calling the nurse with the big orange button on my remote. He asked her for my file with the new results. She rushed off out to her station, returning with a large folder seconds later. I wondered how they had so much information about me from one afternoon, and what it all meant. He asked her to leave and to close the door behind her. What was he going to do to me? He stood up and walked around the room while analysing the papers in the file very carefully. I was trying to read the situation by the expressions on his face, but there weren't any. I interrupted him to tell him I was feeling a lot better. I was. I hoped that he would let me go sooner so I could salvage what was left of the day. Not that I had much else planned. He was so deep into the pages, he didn't respond or even acknowledge what I had said. He finished off sifting through the folder and slammed it shut.

He said he was glad I was feeling better, but that he had to be honest with me and tell me that the results weren't looking great. He tried to soften the blow by flowering his explanation with medical terms, but basically, I had a large, cancerous tumour in my lung. I was a little disappointed that I would have to stay there longer while they took the damn thing out, but was eager for them to get on with it. Apparently, it wasn't that simple. He admitted that in some cases they were able to remove the tumour, but the position of mine, the fact that it had spread, and that I was at stage four meant they wouldn't be able to operate. I was always that rare case. I had found myself on a long, and often unsuccessful road. As I was already at such an advanced stage, Dr. Stafford urged that I start a strong course of chemotherapy. I wouldn't say I was excited, but from how he described it, it seemed like chemo was the cure for cancer. The good thing was that I was young and my body was strong so I would be able to handle it. I was ready to start because the sooner I did it, the sooner I could go to Tennessee.

I asked him exactly how long it would take because I had a ticket to book. He continued explaining the process trying to put it into layman terms, but all I could deduce was that it would take twelve weeks. Twelve weeks? Twelve weeks! They say weeks, so that it doesn't sound too long, but twelve weeks is three months. I thought it would take three days, not a quarter of the year. I couldn't sit around for that long without Madison. I explained my unique situation to him. He was sympathetic but went on to say that it could be even longer. He placed his hand on my shoulder and said that he wasn't really supposed to tell me how long I had left because there was no exact way of calculating, but with the treatment, he could tell me that my body would become so weak, that I wouldn't be able to fly for at least a long while. Insensitive bastard. What did he mean by "how long I had left?" We hadn't even started the treatment and he was already killing me off. And, why would the treatment make me weaker than I was? Wasn't it supposed to do the opposite? No more fluff, I asked him point blank if I was going to die. He was struggling to say no. He danced around for a bit, not making eye contact, and landed on that they would do their very best to make sure I was comfortable. I wanted them to do their very best to save my life. He said that the most important thing was to stay positive. It was hard when he himself didn't seem too sure. At that point, I was a little scared to go home. He stood up and said that I would have to come in for a day every ten days for chemo and that he would come and meet me every other meeting to discuss my progress. Before he left, he disinfected his hands with the antibacterial liquid hanging on the wall near the door. Was I contagious? He said that he would post me some pamphlets with more information. That was it. I had cancer. Within the space of a week, I had reduced from being a healthy young man walking around London with the love of my life to a hospital bed with one foot in the grave.

Physically, I was feeling fine, but as soon as I got home and sat down, I started crying. I knew I shouldn't have gone to the doctor. I bet if they didn't tell me, I would be fine. A part of me still believed that maybe it would all just go away. There would be reports and articles about miracle cases and news of revolutionary treatments that were helping thousands of cancer patients. I was a cancer patient. It was hard to say. I was one of those people in the Cancer Research UK adverts. I had to take control. The only way out was knowledge. I was done with surprises. I read through all the leaflets I was sent from the hospital cover to cover. I researched everything there was to know. I probably knew more about my disease than the doctor himself, but the one thing I couldn't figure out was what to tell Madison. That was when I would stop reading and just stare at the ceiling, sometimes for hours on end. It had felt like a lifetime ago I had seen or heard from her. I found myself day dreaming of our reunion, only to be awakened by the doorbell. Could she have come to surprise me?

It was Will. He was unhappy that I had started locking my door and said that he'd called the hospital a few times, but didn't hear from me.

It was nice that someone was worried. It was surprisingly easy to tell him everything that was going on, and I could tell he was genuinely gutted. He reminded me that he was right next door if I needed absolutely anything anytime even if it was just someone to talk to. I appreciated it, but it was something I would have to figure out and deal with myself. That was the only way I would be able to get a handle on it, and although I wanted to believe that I could beat it, I was always too much of a realist. Plus, it was probably best I started distancing myself from everyone so that it wouldn't hurt as much. There was one person I needed more than ever, though. I sat down to write her a letter. I wanted to tell her everything, but I just didn't know how. What could I tell her? That I was dying? That there was a possibility I would never see her again? Should I have lied and told her that everything was fine? You can only imagine how many scrunched up pieces of paper were launched towards my bin. My aim was getting better, but I was getting nowhere. It was clear I needed to incubate, so I shut up shop for the night.

My eyes sprung open at 4 o'clock in the morning. I don't know if it came to me in my dream, but I knew exactly what I had to write. I had to tell her everything that had happened and how I was feeling. I could talk to her about anything and everything, so I didn't know why I was having such a hard time with it. I didn't want to let her down, but I also didn't want to keep anything from her. It still took me a few attempts to be satisfied with my handwriting, but a few hours later, I had composed the perfect letter. I got back into bed to wait for the post office to open. I woke up again at 4 o'clock, but in the afternoon. I had slept through the whole day. As I was rushing out the door to make it to the post office before it closed, I saw the corner of a pastel blue envelope peeking out of my mailbox. The brown ones were bills, the white ones were not important, but Madison would always use very colourful stationary. I ripped it open to confirm it was from her and took it upstairs to read. I thought I would go to the post office the next morning instead. I made myself a cup of tea, sat back, and let Madison talk to me. She was uncontrollably excited to tell me that some label called Big Machine Records was interested in signing her as an artist. It was fantastic news, I was proud of her, but not very surprised. I knew it was only a matter of time. I couldn't reply with the letter I had written. She was going up, but I was going down. I was scared that I would be holding her back. She deserved better. I couldn't give her what she wanted. Her life was going to be performing concerts at arenas, making speeches at award shows, and as much as I wanted to be there with her, I understood that my time was going to be spent in hospital rooms watching television shows. It was the last thing I wanted to do, but I had to set her free. I was a coward, so for the next few weeks, I went radio silent.

18

The chemo was in full swing, doing its absolute worst. I was throwing up nearly every morning, and I had completely lost my apatite. I didn't want to see anyone, speak to anyone, or do anything. I locked myself away. A nurse would visit me at home three times a week, but there was nothing she could do. Up until then I always considered myself to be quite strong, but the disease systematically knocked me down. Still, as ill as the treatment made me, nothing brought me more pain than not being with my love. I thought about calling her every day, but I had to save her from it all. Nor did I want her to see me withering away. I had lost most of my hair and gained ten years on my face. I didn't want her pity. It was terrifying how quickly it escalated. I was being attacked physically and mentally. It was very difficult to make others understand how I was feeling and to express the kind of thoughts that were going through my mind. Often contemplating suicide. At least then I would have control.

She sent a couple of letters unaware of the situation before I replied with what I feared, but also instructed, would be our last communication. I didn't tell her why, but it was over. It would be easier for her to get over a little heartache than a lifetime of pain if we went deeper. I knew if I told her, she would drop everything and come to my side, but I didn't want her like that. Eventually she would resent me. It was easier to blame it on the distance. I confessed I had never loved like that before, and vowed that I would never love again. It was our final goodbye.

Once the letter had left my hand, I realised I no longer had anything to live for. I told her not to reply, but I secretly hoped that she would. I checked my mail every day, but there was nothing. I filled in what I didn't know. I didn't want her to be angry with me. If only she could know that I was doing it for her. I so badly wanted to send her the previous letter I had written, explaining everything, but I couldn't. I came close a few times, but it would have been selfish. To be safe, I gave it to Will and asked him to post it to her when I passed away. I didn't want to ruin her life, but she deserved to know. I wanted her to know that it was out of my hands. Maybe then she'd forgive me. My condition got exponentially worse, but pain was relative. I didn't feel anything. I was just going through the steps.

Around the time I was starting my second round of a more aggressive therapy, I received an unmarked package. A CD. No sleeve, cover, or note accompanied it, and there was no return address. I ignored it and filed it as spam by chucking it on my coffee table and using it as a coaster. One day, while sitting there doing absolutely nothing else but that, curiosity got the better of me. Boy, am I glad that it did. I put it in my laptop and hit play. A familiarly sad string of notes picked on a guitar played below the voice of my angel. Madison had written and recorded a song for me. I'm not going to sing it because I wouldn't do it justice, but it was entitled, *Forever Only Yours.* It played deep in my heart all day, everyday. It was all I had of her. It was the song I woke up to every morning and the song I fell asleep to.

19

I stop to replay the song in my head. I find it difficult to continue with the story. Chris doesn't let me have my minute. I can see he is hungry to find out what happened next. I gather myself. The barmaid automatically refills our drinks, and asks, "Was that it? Was that the last time you heard from her? Did you reply?"

20

The doctors tried everything. I went through months of chemo and experimental treatments. Because I was young and based in London, Dr. Stafford signed me up for a bunch of clinical trials. I didn't really have faith that any of them would work, but I had nothing to lose. Every now and then I would read about a super food that was the miracle cure for cancer. I ate soursop three times a day every other day for three months, I went through a period where I added a carrot to everything I ate, took a spoon full of hemp seed oil every morning, I even stopped drinking for a while, but that didn't last long. I was so glad when I read that a glass of red wine with lunch and a shot of whiskey before bed were actually good for you. I'm not going to say the treatments got easier because they actually got harder, but I became used to them. There were weeks I was living in Hell on Earth, but then I would randomly have a spell of good days where I could eat, I would want to get out of the house, go for a walk, and even for a short moment feel like I wasn't ill anymore.

The doctor had given me a comprehensive list of things I should and shouldn't eat. I didn't stick to it though. When I did have an appetite, all I wanted was Pizza Hut or McDonald's. Lots of McDonald's. I must give Will a shout out, he would check up on me regularly, bring me food, even DVDs and activities to keep my mind occupied. Bless his heart. Not the Southern definition, which was an insult, I meant it. We were neighbours in the Biblical sense. The good days, however, were always followed by more bad days. I don't like recalling those too much because it was a very dark and miserable time that I never want to revisit. Sometimes I wonder how I made it through. I cannot tell you how many times I came close to ending it early, on my accord. Why would I want to suffer first? Death was inevitable. There was no hope for happiness.

In those mafia movies, when the gangster was held at gunpoint and knew there was no way out, he didn't plead with the gunman not to shoot, he begged for it to be quick. I had my finger on the trigger, but the song Madison recorded for me would always play in my head and keep me from pulling it. I even turned to Jesus to lead me through the darkness.

The weeks turned into months and the months into years, but I was still battling on. Things might have been over between Madison and me, but I thought about her every single day without fail. I missed her so much. I pictured what our lives would have been like if I didn't get ill. A psychotic fantasy that one day we might be together again. I truly believe that was what kept me fighting. Fight, I did. Cancer was no longer my hobby, it was my profession. Most of my days were filled up with all sorts of trials, tests, studies, seminars, and the days that weren't, were spent researching the next. Most of them were free or covered by my insurance, but there were a couple that were extremely expensive. We're talking upwards of £50,000 a year, which was a lot. Luckily, I was in a position where I could afford them. Well, lucky would have been not needing them in the first place, but the doctor told me how important it was to stay positive. I sold the two houses my father had left me and cashed in on the shares I had bought over the years. I was an only child, and didn't have any children of my own, so didn't really have anyone to leave anything to. I thought I'd buy a really rare piece of diamond jewellery that Will could deliver to Madison along with the letter, for all his help and support, I'd leave him my apartment, and if there were anything left, it could go to cancer charities like Macmillan or Cancer Research UK.

21

Four years later, on the first day of June, the first official day of summer in my calendar, I had an appointment with Dr. Stafford to discuss my progress, if there was any. I'd usually go to see him every couple of months after a treatment had completed so that he could tell me that he was surprised at how well I was looking, how strong I was, and that it was a great sign that everything was the same. To me, a good sign would have been that I was getting better, but they were happy I wasn't getting worse. I was just crabbing along. That one time, he called me in during the treatment, and seemed jollier than usual. He proceeded with the results of the treatment I was on at the time, one of the more expensive ones, saying that I wasn't getting worse, but then he hit me with a curveball out of nowhere. He said that there was some good news for once. The treatment was unbelievably effective and the results showed signs of improvement. I sat up in my chair to hear more. He explained that against all expectations, I might be getting better. I mean, I was feeling slightly better. He still wanted to do some further tests, but for the first time, I saw hope in his eyes. Could it be that I was getting my life back? It had been over four years since I had seen Madison, but again, she was the first image that appeared. He was eager to escort me down to the clinic.

He was walking so fast, I was struggling to keep up. There was a real buzz in the ward. At his request, I was given the VIP room, which was more like a suite. He called in a team of maybe eight to ten doctors to examine my most recent scans. I knew a few of them. There was my nutritionist Dr. Li, my treatment consultant Dr. Chakrabarti, one was another consultant I had dealings with, the head nurse, but there were definitely a few serious faces I had never seen before. My doc, the leader, started loudly, saying that he had never heard of, let alone witnessed, a case like mine. The others looked intrigued and huddled closer around my file. I just lay there in the background trying to listen to what they were discussing. It was strange. They were talking about me like I wasn't there. Every now and then, one of them would look over at me, and then go back to the circle. I tried to raise my neck like a meerkat to see what they were all so engrossed in, but I was too far. Their faces weren't giving much away either. Doctors would be good poker players.

They must have talked for close to an hour before my doctor adjourned the council. Some of them left the room, but a couple that I knew stuck around. Dr. Stafford looked concerned. He sat down at the end of my bed and asked me how I was feeling. A redundant question. Honestly, I was on one of my good stretches, which were no longer so few and far between, but was still dreading the inevitable dive of the rollercoaster I was on. He pointed at some dots and shadows on one of the scans. He tried explaining what I was looking at, but I could never make heads or tails of those things. I would just smile, nod, and pretend I could see what he was seeing. He started explaining it to me medically first, but when I didn't respond with the reaction he was expecting, he broke it down for me.

My new scans showed that the treatment was working tremendously and that if I completed it, there would be little to no trace of the disease left in my system. I nodded inattentively while I processed exactly what he was saying. It took a few seconds to sink in, but once I realise there was no *but*, I wrapped my arms around him. I wasn't much of a hugger, but it was a reaction I didn't have time to control. The other doctors came in closer and one by one put their hands on my shoulder before leaving the room. There was a tear in my eye. My first question was whether I was clear to fly. He knew exactly why I was asking. After the treatment, which ran for another two weeks, he encouraged me to live a full life and do whatever I felt up to. He warned that I was still at very high risk of the disease coming back, but as far as he was concerned, they wouldn't be trying anything further, so I should accept and fully enjoy the gift I had been given. I was to call him immediately if I was feeling unwell, and he still wanted to see me before Christmas for a progress report, but that was it. Dr. Stafford got up and left. I was free from the prison but needed a few minutes to gather myself. I was alive again. I felt so much better than I had that morning, proving that a lot of it was psychological. I was excited, not because my life expectancy had just multiplied, but because it meant I could see Madison again. To be honest, I was also excited to go home and tell Will.

22

The day after my treatment was done, I was on a plane to my beloved Tennessee. I thought I'd surprise Madison and explain everything in person. I had worked through all the possible scenarios. The one I was hoping for the most was that she went out with a couple of other people, realised that none of them were me, was currently single, ecstatic to see me, and we could pick up where we left off all those years ago. Unlikely I know, but if I had learned anything, it was that miracles do happen. However, I did try and prepare myself for the great possibility that she was angry at me, had fallen in love with someone else, or worse, was married. The whole flight there, I practiced what I was going to say, how I was going to say it, and even planned where. My five-hour layover in Minneapolis - Saint Paul International Airport gave me enough time to eat something and freshen up. I changed my shirt, washed my face, styled my hair, brushed my teeth, and put some cologne on at duty-free. I wanted to be ready to go and see her as soon as I landed but didn't want to arrive on her doorstep looking like I had just stepped off a twelve-hour flight.

On the second leg, in the tiny plane, the captain told us that we were expecting some mild turbulence, so would have to remain seated with our seatbelt fastened for most of the flight. I wasn't too bothered as there wasn't enough room for me to stand up straight anyway. The plane started to shake. Mild turbulence, my foot. Mild maybe for a jumbo jet, but we were in a toy plane. The rattling of silverware in the trolley made it worse. The pilot swung the plane left and right like a child with his arms out running around the playground. Suddenly, the lights went off and the engine went silent. It was like the pilot had pulled out the key. My feet tightened as I felt the plane free falling. I looked around. Everyone was secretly starting to freak out. How ironic it would have been if I died in a plane wreck on my way to see Madison. After all that. A few stretched seconds later, the pilot got control of the aircraft again. The lights came on, the turbulence settled, and complete calm was restored. I unclenched and pretended like I wasn't terrified half to death.

I was the first one up as soon as we landed. It was getting late in the evening, so I rushed out of the airport and got straight into a taxi. There wasn't any time to waste. I wanted to reach her house at an appropriate time. In the cab, I ran through my lines and the correct response to every possible outcome for the final time. Her street was familiar, but there was something about her house that looked a bit different. I couldn't figure out whether it was the landscaping, if they had repaved the driveway, the colour of the garage door, or all three. It had been a long time. I double-checked that the taxi dropped me off at the right address, as I saw it drive away. I took a deep breath and straightened up. I walked up the steps onto the porch, took another moment to gather my nerves, and knocked on the door. I was prepared with what to say if her parents opened the door but hadn't factored in if she wasn't at home. I couldn't see her car in the driveway, but that was probably because it was in the mega-garage. I waited a minute, but there was no answer. I saw a light on in one of the upstairs windows, so knocked again. An excruciatingly long wait later, the hall light came on and a man answered the door. He looked too young to be her father, and a lot more Chinese than I had remembered from the pictures I had seen. He stared at me blankly, waiting to talk. I leaned back to triple check the numbers on the side of the door. I was definitely at the right house. The inside looked familiar, but different too. It through me off, but I managed to eventually ask him if Madison was home. What if she had married a middle-aged Chinese man, I feared. That would have been awkward. The vacant look on his face didn't vacate. I repeated, but again, no response. He shook his head and slammed the door in my face. I stood there with my nose against the door trying to piece together what had just happened and then knocked again. The man opened, only slightly, with the exact same look on his face. I thought I was in The Twilight Zone. I asked again, "Madison Edwards?" He thought for a second and then smiled. In a surprisingly southern accent, he informed me that The Edwards had moved out nearly three years ago. I asked if he knew where they moved to, if they had left a forwarding address, anything, but he couldn't help. He slammed the door in my face before I could think of any more questions to ask him. Shit! That was one scenario I didn't plan for. Defeated, I rolled my suitcase to the bottom of the drive and sat on it, while I planned my next move.

The first thing I needed to do was to get a cab to take me to a hotel. Easier said than done especially because I was in the middle of nowhere and my phone decided to stop working. Typical. I couldn't bother the Chinese man again, so I thought I'd try and walk to the main road, and find a payphone, or a bar, shop, anything.

I set off down the long quiet residential boulevard dragging my suitcase behind me. The wheels were obnoxiously loud as they rolled down the street. I was worried I was going to wake up the whole street. I didn't know exactly where I was going, but I remembered that we'd driven in that direction before. I must have walked for a good forty-five minutes, trying to recall the way with every step. I was admiring the large houses, guesstimating how cheap they were in comparison to properties in London. There was a spectacular white house on the corner that was slightly larger than the others. I noticed a lawn sign out front, but it was dark so I couldn't see what it said. I walked closer to take a look, instantly being rewarded for finding The Brentwood Inn. By a stroke of luck, I had found myself at a bed and breakfast. Most of the lights were off, but there was a bulb on the porch that was struggling to stay lit. I walked towards it to investigate. If it were a hotel, then maybe they'd have a phone that I could use. There was a "vacancy" sign penned on lined notepad paper stuck to the door. Professional. I dragged my suitcase up the stairs and rang the doorbell. While it was still playing out the tune to Rocky Top, a large older lady let me in. She turned the lights on to reveal hundreds of cat figurines dotted around the room. She walked behind the counter and welcomed me formally. She seemed friendly, but also a little apprehensive. Not that she couldn't handle a strange man walking in that late. Before enquiring about a room, I asked whether I could use a phone. I thought if Madison picked up, I wouldn't have to stay there. The lady pulled one of those old rotary dial phones up from under the desk. I had never used one of them before and quickly became frustrated at how long it took me to dial Madison's number. The phone was not connecting, so I asked the lady for her assistance. She received the same dead tone and concluded that either the number was wrong or it had been disconnected. I was sure the number was right and was hoping that it was just a fault with her ancient phone. I had no choice but to get a room for the night and try again in the morning. The room was unspectacular but clean. It felt more like I was staying in a friend's guest room than a hotel room. It was cheap, close, and getting late so I couldn't complain. I had bigger things to worry about. That was the only number I had for Madison. She had moved away and her phone was disconnected. How was I going to find her? What would my next move be? Was that it?

23

Another punter at the bar calls over Ashley to place his order. She is obviously annoyed and makes me promise not to continue without her. Chris pushes, dying to know if I found Madison. I take a long sip of my drink. I'm slowly approaching my limit, but signal for her to fill me up too. I'll need another drink to get through the next bit…

24

I asked around, but no one knew anything. I showed the landlady a picture of Madison, asking if she knew the Edwards that used to live in the neighbourhood, but she couldn't help either. She did however suggest that I check the phone book to see if maybe she was listed. A phonebook? I had heard people say, "If you're ever in town, look me up," but had never heard of anyone who actually went somewhere and looked someone up. To be honest, I didn't really understand how phonebooks worked. Was I to believe that they had everyone's name, address, and telephone number out there for anyone to see? I quickly learned that Edwards was an extremely popular surname in that town. I eliminated all the Drs, Frs, Revs and all the ones without the initials of either her, her mum, or dad, but was still left with a list of over ten. I asked the lady if I could use her phone again, sat down, and started making my enquiries. It didn't take more than twenty minutes for my dreams to be crushed. I was running out of moves fast, but I had no intention of giving up.

I walked back in the direction of her house, knocking on all of her neighbour's doors. I don't know where I conjured up the courage, but I was on a mission. The best information I got was from an old lady who lived opposite that told me everything I already knew. It was hopeless. I had failed. I was beaten. The world wasn't as small and connected as they made it out to be. I didn't know what my next play was. It wasn't supposed to go down like that. The belief in my heart was fading.

25

The more time I spent in the South without my Belle, the less time I wanted to spend there. It just didn't feel right without her. I was only there for her and she wasn't there. Deflated, I checked out of the B&B and ordered a taxi back to the airport. The driver wanted to talk, but I was in no mood. There was traffic like you couldn't imagine. Apparently, the President was in town that day, so all the roads were blocked off. Even the president of the United States was in town, but there was no sign of Madison. My flight to London wasn't confirmed, so I wasn't in any immediate rush, but I needed to get out. Everything there reminded me of her. I had my head resting against the window spotting and reminiscing of the places we had been together. The restaurants we ate at, the Walmart, the Sonic, the café with the horrible tea, the bar where her friend worked, the road that led to the house I rented. Wait! The bar where her friend worked. That was it. How could I have been so stupid? Without much hesitation, I yelled at the driver to stop the taxi, turn around, and take me to the bar. He must have thought I was an alcoholic because it was 9:30 in the morning. That was my last chance. Her friend, Britney, would know how I could find Madison.

I paid the taxi driver and rolled my suitcase to the door. It was closed. Shit! It opened at 11 a.m. so I sat on my suitcase and waited for it to open. It was unpleasantly hot that particular morning. The sun was shining directly on me and there was no escape to shade. Sitting in one place in the blistering heat for an hour and a half doing absolutely nothing felt like five hours. Eventually a man with a large set of clinking keys walked towards me and opened up. He made a snarky little comment about how early I was. I could tell he didn't mean it in a mean way though and was just joking around. I needed him to be nice because he would be able to give me information about Britney. I lifted up my suitcase and followed him in.

A few minutes late, the barmaid, a pretty little thing, walked in. No, it wasn't Britney. She asked what she could get me. I wasn't there for a drink, but I thought I ought to order one, hoping that would make them want to help me more. As soon as she brought me my Jack, I enquired whether Britney still worked there. She tilted her head to the side and scrunched her nose. Nope. I couldn't tell if she genuinely didn't know a Britney, or she was concerned I was a stalker. There were too many reasons for her not to tell me, so I told her more. She swung her ponytail the other way and said that no one called Britney had worked there since she'd been there. Better, but I was there for answers. She continued that she hadn't been working there for that long, so wasn't the best person to ask. I looked towards the back to see if the man who opened up, who I assume was the manager, could come out to help me. She yelled out, "Hey John, do you know a Britney?"

The man walked out carrying a box of bottled beers, placed it on the counter, thought for a second, and answered, "No." He turned to look at me. I explained that she worked there four years ago and that I had lost touch with her and was trying to reconnect. He raised his eyebrows, concerned. He informed me that the bar had changed ownership, so he wouldn't have any of her records on file, and even if he did, he wouldn't give them out to random guys off the street who came in looking for any of his barmaids. I assured him I wasn't a serial killer, but he didn't know that for sure. I understood that he was doing it to protect them, but I needed something, anything. He told the barmaid, Stephanie, to fill up the beer and came around the counter to sit next to me. He believed my story, so quietly told me that the girls had a very quick turnaround because they were usually either working there for the summer break until they found a career, or they were aspiring country singers and made it big. He was obviously listing what had happened to his previous employees. He looked over at his current, who was squatted down filling the fridge wondering where she'd end up.

He apologised that he wasn't able to help. Stephanie, who had been useless up until that point stood up and said that Manuel, one of the guys who used to work in the kitchen, had been there for like nine years. I looked at the man for confirmation. His smile assured me that Manuel was my best, and only, option. I looked back towards the kitchen area, but no one was there. The manager got up and walked back around the counter. He pulled out a laminated sheet from underneath the till to check the timetable. I was in luck. Manuel didn't usually work Saturdays, but was scheduled to come in at 3 p.m. because there was an open mic night event that day. It was barely past 11 a.m. and I had nowhere to go, but to hang out with my best friend Jack Daniel.

Time was being measured by drinks. The bar was pretty full by lunchtime. Loud groups occupied the tables surrounding me, so I was kept entertained by their conversations. A few more girls joined the bar. I sensed that Stephanie was filling in the later shift with all the gossip. 3 o'clock arrived, but there was no sign of Manuel. Not that I would have recognised him, but I was under the impression the manager would introduce me to him. Twenty minutes late, but he did show up. Stephanie walked him over and filled him in on who I was. He was a scruffy guy, but that didn't have anything to do with anything. I told him I was looking for a girl called Britney and asked if he remembered her. He was quick to shake his head. That wasn't good enough. He didn't even try. I told him it was very important and to think very carefully. I doubted he stayed in touch with her, but maybe he could give me a nugget of information, a clue, that would help me in what was quickly becoming a wild goose chase. He rolled his eyes up and to the right for a few seconds, and then came back with that he remembered the name, but couldn't place a face. He started justifying his response, worried that he was in trouble. He couldn't help me, so I dismissed him. Nobody could help me.

Stephanie was sorry and poured me a pity drink on the house. I had failed, and there really were no more leads to follow up on. It was officially time to start drinking my sorrows away. Beating cancer didn't matter, as there was no life without Madison. There is no chemo for a broken heart.

Eddie King

26

Performers took the stage to sing about love and heartbreak, but they knew nothing of it. Most of them were pretty terrible, but my glass was full, and I had nowhere else to go. The cheering was getting too much. They would clap and whistle to welcome the next act on stage, then again when the act introduced themselves, and again when they talked about the song they were going to sing, and then again after the first line, and then again at the end of the performance, and then again for the next act who played another song I had never heard. It was a vicious cycle of clapping, and if you didn't join in, they would think you were a monster that didn't support local talent. I decided to stay for one final drink before making my way to the airport where I would take the first flight to anywhere in Europe. To Stephanie's amazement,

I downed the generous glass of whiskey. I threw all the dollars scrunched up in my pocket, giving her a very handsome tip, grabbed the handle of my suitcase, and stood up to leave.

As soon as I got up, I heard something familiar. I recognised the song from the first string plucked. I had heard that song before. A hit? It wasn't until the first word that I made the connection. It was the song. The song. It was the song Madison wrote. For me. A wave of complete and utter happiness rushed through my body, and my heart started thumping out of my chest. I looked over at the stage, and there she was. As beautiful as ever. Madison was standing right there. I was in shock. I had to look away, take a deep breath to make sure I wasn't hallucinating. I stood right in front of her, making sure what I was seeing was real. As soon as I caught her eye, she froze. The whole bar was silent. I dropped my suitcase to the ground and took a few giant steps forward. She took her guitar off, moved the microphone out of the way, and jumped off the stage. We locked. A long kiss, followed by hundreds of little kisses. The crowd clapped and whistled. The host hopped on stage and called an interval. Everyone dispersed, but we were stood there as one.

I was broken by emotion. My knees were weak, so I grabbed her hand and we sat down back at the bar. I didn't want to wait for a second more and told her everything. I told her I had never loved anyone as much and came looking for her. She was flooding with tears. She was struggling, but told me that her parents had moved back to California, and wanted her to go with them, but she wanted to stay in Nashville. She played the song at every open mic night in town, hoping that one day it would reach my ears. She told me that she was hurt when I didn't reply to her letters, but never stopped loving me for a single minute. She hadn't gone out with anyone ever since and hoped every day that I would come and find her. She never gave up on me. That was one scenario I couldn't have even dreamed to imagine. I couldn't stop staring at her. I just had to look at her. She had her hair in a waterfall braid, her eyes still had that sparkle and, of course, she had her cowboy boots on.

From that day on, we didn't leave each other's side. We were together always. We got married a week later at The Hermitage Hotel. It was a beautiful ceremony. Will and a few of my other friends flew out from London. I moved to Tennessee, we had a couple of daughters, who both got married and are living out of state, a dog, a house in Franklin with a white picket fence. There were ups and downs like in every relationship, but we never fought, never argued, and never got upset with each other because we knew how rubbish life was apart.

27

Chris raises his glass in celebration, but unfortunately that wasn't the end of the story…

Eddie King

28

We were old and had lived a full life together. I got old a lot sooner than her, but she kept me feeling young. She cooked healthy meals, took me for long walks, and didn't let me get lazy. Once the kids went off to college, we travelled the world, we went to Singapore, India, China, all over Europe, but I liked it most when we were home in Westhaven, Franklin, Tennessee.

One morning, we woke up late. I woke up first, so I went to the kitchen to put the kettle on. I called out to wake her up, but she wasn't responding. I walked back to the room, but she wasn't there. I looked around and found her sitting on the porch swing with the duvet around her shoulders. As soon as I sat down beside her the kettle started whistling. She offered to go and make the tea, but that was always my job. It was my only job. I shuffled in, still half asleep. I opened the cabinet, and I don't know how, I knocked a cup off the shelf. It fell to the ground and smashed everywhere. Just my luck. I yelled out to let her know I was fine. I made the tea, walked half way to the door, and then turned around back to the kitchen. I yelled again asking if she wanted a biscuit but didn't hear anything back. I balanced a couple on top of the cups and slowly made my way out again. I proudly made it to the porch, bragging of my achievement. I sat beside her, put our teas on the little table in front, and told her I got her a biscuit anyway. I thought she had fallen asleep, so I nudged her, but she wasn't waking up. I shook her harder, but nothing. My love was gone. I took hold of her hand, and begged the Lord to take me. She had left me. I always thought that I would have been the one to go first. Every year, for the last six, on the anniversary of the first day we met, on her birthday, on our wedding anniversary, and today, the day I found her again at this very bar, I come to celebrate our time together. I think about her every day and carry her picture around wherever I go.

Eddie King

29

Ashley is not holding back and lets her tears flow freely. Like myself, I can see Chris trying to hold back. He tells me that it was both the happiest and saddest story he has ever heard. He puts his hand on my shoulder to comfort me. I reiterate that the moral of the story is to never give up, and that if he really loved the girl he followed to Tennessee, and she loved him back, it will work out. He came over and started talking to me to try and cheer up an old man drinking alone at a bar staring at a photo of his wife, but left with a lot more. I take my final sip for my angel, my queen, my Southern Girl.

CPSIA information can be obtained at www.ICGtesting.com
Printed in the USA
LVOW08s0032061215

465566LV00003B/13/P